The Onyx Ring

Family Relics Book 2

by

Tanya Miranda

The Onyx Ring
By Tanya Miranda

Copyright © 2018 Tanya Miranda

Print Edition

Cover by Seedlings Design Studio
www.seedlingsonline.com

Published by Blue Dragonfly Publishing
www.bluedragonflypublishing.com

ISBN-13: 978-1-7323919-0-1
ISBN-10: 1-7323919-0-4

For Ryan & Roman,
I am still enchanted by your magic.

THE ELDER'S VISION

Ryland's cup of coffee shatters into a million irreparable pieces as it hits the ceramic floor. Detailed images of the recent past crystallize in his mind in a matter of seconds, shocking his senses. He stares out the window with his mouth ajar, holding his breath.

Oregon turns with a startled glance. Stepping off a footstool in front of a tall bookshelf across the room, Oregon takes a step toward him. "Are you alright, my lord?"

No response.

Oregon repeats his question, and Ryland snaps out of his daze. He bends down and stares at the tiny porcelain pieces swimming in the spilled coffee on the floor. "Finally," Ryland whispers.

Oregon pushes a packed metal book cart with his old, weak arms toward Ryland at the window. Each slow step creates a *shush* that rings in unison with the *squeak* of the cart's wheels. When he arrives at Ryland's side, he stares up at his master with eager eyes. "Have you seen something?"

Ryland nods. "Several days ago, I felt a supernatural ripple from across the globe, but I couldn't decipher its source. The leaves on my Rowan tree fluttered with nerves, as did the old oaks in the garden. Yet, they told me nothing. But now, the visions have finally come."

"About those dragons on the news?"

"Yes."

"I knew it would come to you eventually." Oregon releases a sigh of satisfaction. "Tell me, what have you seen?"

Ryland's index finger taps his upper lip as his other arm crosses his chest. "From what I understand of Finna's coven's laws of magic, the powers of a sorceress are transferred to only one heir of her choosing. It seems that Agatha decided not to pass on her magic and died without choosing an heir. Yet, her two granddaughters, Jasmyn and Katarina, the two girls in the news footage, received her powers. It's odd. In the visions, Agatha's coven sisters seemed perplexed. They didn't understand how it happened. Even though she didn't choose an heir, her magic passed on to her kin."

As Ryland pauses to stare out the window, Oregon lifts one of the three thick, leather-bound books from the book cart and places them upon Ryland's table. The edges of the brown leather cover are black from centuries of use. Dull stains mark the metal knob where a rope holds the book shut.

Oregon dusts off the first book with a handkerchief. "Magic is the ruler of its own destiny."

Ryland cocks his head at Oregon. "What did you say?"

"Right here, on the cover of *Book of Sol*, it is etched, 'Magic is the ruler of its own destiny.'" Oregon chuckles. "I believe I'm translating it correctly."

As Ryland stares at the cover of the ancient book, a crooked smile lights up his face. *Loritida, you conniving witch. Stealing that book from Finna was the smartest thing you ever did.*

Although he's read that line many times over in his eight centuries of studying magic all over the world, including in several dozen clans and covens of sorcery, this is the first time he feels its full meaning. Like Mother Nature and the chaotic wonder that is the universe, magic decides its own destiny.

2

After setting two more books on the table, Oregon removes his robe and lays it over the back of a wooden chair lined with brown-stained leather upholstery. Ryland paces away from the table while Oregon prepares the books for use.

With his bony, withered hands moving in a jagged motion, Oregon dusts the leather covers with a damp cloth and then unwinds the twine around each knob. "What else did you see in your visions?"

"The confusion led to the granddaughters accidentally releasing the Gregorn Dragons from their prison."

Oregon pauses his dusting the second book. "How does one 'accidentally' release a prisoner from an enchanted prison?"

"It seems that, while holding the dragons' entrapment case, Katarina recited the spell from the *Book of Whispers*."

"Did she know nothing of the consequences?"

"No! She and Jasmyn knew nothing of Agatha's magic or their inheritance. Agatha kept it secret from them. Katarina thought she was reciting a poem."

Oregon leans back in his chair with his mouth agape. "A poem…"

"But, reciting the spell was only half of the enchantment. You see, to release the dragons from their prison and still maintain control over them, Katarina had to open the entrapment case herself. The spell wasn't complete without that last step."

Oregon unwinds the rope closure of the second book. "If she didn't open the entrapment case, then how were the dragons released?"

"Moments after Katarina read the spell, Jasmyn took the box which held the souls and destroyed it, completing the spell—in a way."

Oregon tilts his head. "What do you mean?"

"A sorceress can release the dragons under her control so

long as she possesses the enchantment case. But, Jasmyn destroyed the case and thereby destroyed her control over them."

"And all hell broke loose on the west coast of the United States, as the news media reported."

"Secrets such as these often lead to chaos."

Oregon nods. "So, if they were unaware of their powers, how did they make that last dragon in the desert disappear?"

As he paces alongside the length of the long wooden table, rubbing his hands in concentration, Ryland pieces the scenes from his visions together. "Once they became aware of their powers, Jasmyn and Katarina attempted to entrap the dragons, but neither girl was able to execute the entrapment spell successfully."

"Because the magic was split between them?"

"That's my guess."

"Then what did they do?"

Ryland shrugs his shoulders and shakes his head. "I can only assume that once Katarina died, all of Agatha's powers transferred to Jasmyn. She then recited the entrapment spell, and the last dragon disappeared. The visions aren't always complete; sometimes I have to formulate my own conclusions."

"Amazing, the power of secrets." Oregon furrows his eyebrows. "That other sorceress on the news… it seemed as if her powers had no effect on the dragon. Is she not as powerful as Jasmyn?"

"Patricia? Oh no, she is a very powerful sorceress." With his hand folded across his chest, Ryland walks over to the bay window and stares down at the plaza where the fountain of a goddess stands in the bright sunlight. Ryland sighs as he recalls long-forgotten memories.

"When Finna created her army of dragons, she made these three dragons indestructible. Only their own dragonkind

4

can kill them." Ryland huffs, a wry smile appearing on his face. "It was a clever move on Finna's part. She knew the Foreman Clan's magic surpassed her coven's powers. The dragons practically annihilated the Foreman Clan."

"And those hideous creatures in the news, that looked part human. Did Finna create those as well?"

"No. Those are the villagers from the Isle of Enid. The dragons put a spell on them to give them unnatural strength, and they fought alongside the dragons against the Foreman Clan's army of soldiers."

"But, they look so monstrous."

Ryland stares out the window once more. "They didn't always look that way. They transformed when the dragons rebelled against the coven. It's a product of abusing dark magic."

Oregon untwists the tie of the third book, then leans back in his chair to massage his weary hands. "How so?"

"Dark magic gauges the caster's worthiness." Ryland paces away from the window. "Many sorcerers aren't worthy and don't dare attempt to use it. Many have a false sense of righteousness and easily fall victim to the darkness. If your intentions are greedy or evil, using dark magic will consume you, and the outcome is unpredictable.

"The Gregorn Dragons were created with dark magic, and therefore their magic follows the same rules. When the dragons revolted against the coven, their intentions were selfish. So, the dark magic rebelled against them. All their dragon kin grew weak, and the coven's magic destroyed them easily. The dragons' loyal villagers became gruesome beasts."

Oregon nods and then shakes his head. "In all my years working with you, I've never seen such creatures. And I've seen plenty of sights that would make the bravest tremble with fear."

"Oregon, my old friend, the seventy years that I've

5

known you isn't nearly enough to learn of all the magical species, clans, and covens that exist around the world—the good and evil, lovely and horrifying. Magic comes in all shades." Ryland smiles as he walks back to the window.

"That it does." Oregon chuckles. "And although you have shown me many things, I still get frightened by these particular *shades* of magic." Oregon releases a long, thoughtful sigh. "Perhaps fear comes with age. Magic is for the young and brave."

Ryland glances back at Oregon. "Don't count yourself out of the game, my old friend. You have many years left in you."

"Time consumes us all. I've been lucky to reach this far, and I'll be even luckier when God decides it's time for me to join him in heaven." Oregon sucks in an embarrassed breath. He adjusts himself in his seat. "I'm sorry, my lord. I didn't mean to offend."

"There's no need to apologize. It's not your fault that time can never consume me. You didn't trap me in this youthful form to helplessly watch my oldest friend age before my eyes and one day die in front of me. As for heaven, well, not even with all my centuries of study can I offer an alternate theory of the afterlife. Between the two of us, you are the more fortunate on that account."

Ryland looks back out the window and down at the fountain goddess holding her hands up in the air. Her face is serene with her mouth slightly open, as if singing a delightful tune to the skies, and her stone dress flows down her form as if the wind is moving it. A youthful creature frozen in time.

The pigeons wading in the fountain's pool dash upwards into the air and swirl in a spiral pattern, drawing Ryland's attention upwards. The flock's tight formation creates a thick blanket of dark gray in the sky, as if they are holding onto each other, fluttering in unison until they fly east and out of Ryland's view.

Such simplicity. Such freedom. Beautiful, wondrous freedom.

"What are we researching today?" Oregon asks, opening the first book on the table. It groans as the stiff leather spine bends back.

"Manipulation of the entrapment spell, details of the Forbidden Consumption, and the possibility of repeating the coven's time-reversal spell. Now that Caderyn and Kean know of the existence of the dragon and of Finna's kin, it seems they are in need of this knowledge."

A furrow appears in Oregon's eyebrows. "What does Caderyn plan to do with the dragon?"

"With a force of nature that strong, whatever Caderyn wants."

SKETCHES

A forceful pounding on the front door of the apartment awakens Jasmyn from her dream. She grunts when she rises from her bed, her muscles aching as she pulls herself up to her feet. After this morning's exercise in the desert, executing elemental spells that nearly knocked her out cold, Jasmyn's entire body is stiff, begging for more rest. She adjusts her brown T-shirt and wipes her face before opening the door.

She inhales deeply when she sees Brian's smile. "Did I wake you?" He walks in, several plastic bags in each hand.

Jasmyn nods and rubs her eyes.

"Any luck this time?"

"No. Kat still won't speak to me in my dreams."

"Maybe you're just tired." He places the bags on the floor and shuts the door. "You've been working on those spells every day."

"I feel like I've enrolled in a boot camp workout. I've never been so exhausted."

He points at her arms and widens his eyes. "Whoa. Look at your muscles."

Jasmyn raises her arms and flexes her muscles. A sideways smirk flickers across her face.

"You're ripped."

After a few seconds, Jasmyn lowers her arms into a self-embrace, presses her lips into a tight line, and glances to the side.

"It's okay to smile, you know."

"I know, but," Jasmyn sighs, "it's hard to keep smiling."

She stares down at the kitchen floor tiles, losing herself in the disconcerting details of her most recent dream. She recalls opening her mouth to speak to Katarina, being unable to produce a single sound, and Katarina staring intently but not talking.

And no matter how hard Jasmyn fights it, thoughts of Katarina inevitably remind her of how she is responsible for her sister's death, and how her family has abandoned her because of it. Although it was Jasmyn's decision to not return home after Katarina's death, no one has come looking for her either.

It's best this way—living separately. I don't deserve their love, and my presence would only remind them.

When Brian lifts the plastic bags onto the counter, it breaks Jasmyn's bout of self-loathing.

"I found a place in town that sells art supplies, close to the market," Brian says as he pulls out a box of cereal.

"Froot Loops?"

"Of course, for strong muscles." He slams a gallon of milk onto the counter. "For strong bones."

Jasmyn smirks.

"Here it is." He hands Jasmyn a black, hardcover book. "They didn't have journals, but they did have sketchbooks. Maybe it's better. Since your dreams are so elaborate, maybe you could draw them."

With eager hands, Jasmyn grabs the small book and flips through the blank pages all the way to the end. She glances back up at Brian and stares at him with longing eyes as he puts away the rest of the groceries. She notices the way he mouths the words "peanut butter" and "jelly" before he puts the jars in the cupboard, and how he whispers each cold-cut meat's name as he places them in the fridge. When he's finished, he stands across the counter from Jasmyn with his hands on his hips.

"What?" He glances at the book in her hands and then back up to her eyes. "It's no good?"

Jasmyn looks down at the sketchbook. "It's perfect. Thank you."

Brian settles onto a stool opposite Jasmyn as she bends the spine of the sketchbook so far back that the book stays open without effort. She twirls a fine gel pen in one hand, and ideas rattle through her mind.

"Well," Brian begins, "if you're up to it, I found a lake we could visit if—" Brian pauses, mesmerized by the confident flow of her pen.

Jasmyn sketches the outline of a little girl's frame in several long strokes. With smaller, sharper whips of the pen, she fills in the details of the dress, with its lace trim and a rose petal print on the skirt. Wind pulls part of the skirt's hem upwards. She spins the book to a new angle and scratches fervently, filling in the wavy strands in the little girl's hair.

Another turn of the book, and with the drawing upside down, Jasmyn fills in shadows on the ground and along the right side of standing figure. After a few more minutes, she sits back and wrinkles her nose in moderate satisfaction.

"That's Katarina on the cliff, looking at the sunset," she says as she turns the book to Brian.

Brian stares at the drawing with his mouth open. "I... I can't believe how quickly you drew that. Were you going to major in art at Berkeley?"

"Civil Engineering." Jasmyn spins the book back, turns two pages, and draws on a fresh page. "When I was small, I loved the artwork in the *Book of Whispers*. But when I couldn't look at the artwork anymore, I started drawing. I became quite good at castles and mountain landscapes."

"Why couldn't you look at the artwork?"

"Nana stopped reading to me and spent all her time reading to Kat. She loved the *Book of Whispers*. Kat never let it go." Jasmyn shrugs her shoulders as she continues sliding her pen across the page. "I guess something good came from all of that."

Jasmyn swallows hard, forcing herself out of that familiar pit of bitterness. Any of Nana's and Katarina's crimes against her—however major or minor—have all been paid for by their demise.

Death is the ultimate atonement.

"So how did drawing castles lead to civil engineering?"

Jasmine lifts her pen from the page and stares up into the air for a second, eyes narrowed. "Once, when Kat was really little, about four-years-old, she got sick and was stuck in bed for weeks. Mom, Dad, and Nana were out talking to doctors, and I was left to babysit. I was told to stay in her room the whole time, so I took my sketchbook in there with me."

She lifts the pen to shake it, blots the felt tip on a napkin on the counter, and resumes drawing.

"Kat asked me to draw her a castle. She liked it so much that she asked me to draw mountains. And then a bridge. And then a church, and so on. By the end of the day, I'd drawn an entire town with a school, a park, a highway and everything. I even drew townspeople, old ladies with canes, little kids playing in the park and riding bicycles, and dogs on leashes. I filled the sketchbook with something like sixty drawings, at least."

Jasmyn pauses and glances to the side. "I wonder where that sketchbook is now."

Brian grins as Jasmyn's bemused expression changes back to one of fond memory.

"She even asked me to draw a cemetery. I was like, 'Why a cemetery?' and Kat said, 'For the dead people, of course.'

Seemed logical. So, I drew a cemetery."

"That's pretty mature for a four year old."

"Daisies, dandelions, and rose bushes... it was more like a flower garden with a couple of tombstones than a grave site. But, it was Kat's little village, so I drew what she wanted. It made her feel better."

"*You* made her feel better." Brian stares intently at Jasmyn.

Jasmyn shrugs her shoulders. "We had some nice moments, but they were few and far between." She finishes her drawing and spins the book around to show Brian. "Her favorite was this bridge I drew. She called it The Golden Kat Bridge. I promised her I would one day build it for her. So, from then on, I've always wanted to build bridges."

Brian lifts his eyebrows and exhales as he gazes upon Jasmyn's art. He gawks at the gorgeous drawing of a bridge over a body of water, complete with lions roaring at the entrance gate and cars driving past them. Mountains loom in the distance as the sun sets over a peak. The ripple in the water seems to glisten in Brian's eyes. "Wow. It's... wow."

The compliment warms Jasmyn's cheeks, and the corners of her lips turn upwards. It only takes seconds before she realizes that even if she were to become an engineer and build a bridge and call it The Golden Kat Bridge, her sister would never see it. She fights the sadness, as she's been doing every day since Kat died, and buries it behind a straight face.

You don't deserve to be sad. You don't deserve to be happy. Just be, for now.

"You know," Brian says, "this Golden Kat Bridge is a great start for this journal. It made you smile for a second, and you remembered your sister being happy." He stands and digs his hands into his jean pockets. "Maybe, if you remember Kat that way, whatever is keeping you and her from talking in your dreams might change."

Jasmyn looks up at him with a squint.

"Maybe," Brian swallows, still staring at Jasmyn, "if you stop punishing yourself while you're awake, maybe your subconscious will follow."

Lowering her gaze, she places the pen inside the fold of a clean page and closes the sketchbook. *He doesn't understand. He will never understand.*

She presses her lips together and stands. "Thank you for the sketchbook," she says without looking at Brian.

"I'm sorry, Jaz. I didn't mean to…"

With the book in her hand, she walks to her bedroom and shuts the door.

3

NEW ENCOUNTERS

The incessant doorbell echoes throughout the house, and Logan rushes downstairs in his pajamas. "I'm coming!" he yells as he careens toward the front door. The ringing stops. He peeks through the window and furrows his eyebrows at a tall, lanky man dressed in a posh gray suit suitable for an afternoon wedding. His blond hair is slicked back, and thin-rimmed glasses sit on the angular bridge of his nose.

Logan opens the screen door and narrows his eyes at the man through the glass of the closed front door. "Can I help you?"

"Good afternoon, young Logan. My name is Arsen. I would like to speak to you regarding your late grandmother, Agatha. May I come in?"

With thicker doubt brewing in his mind, Logan stands tall and straightens his back. He folds his arms over his chest as he studies the stranger from head to toe. "What do you have to do with my grandmother?"

Arsen smiles grandly. "It seems that your grandmother may have some artifacts that belong to my family. We've been searching for them for quite some time. May I come in?"

A glimmer of sunlight sparkles off something around the man's neck, and Logan focuses on a medallion hanging from a silver necklace that peeks through the open collar of his white button-up shirt. Logan remembers the enchanted charm Patricia gave him to ward off spells from other sorcerers, a charm he's kept around his neck ever since.

Arsen takes a step closer to the front door. "Please, Logan, allow me to come in so that I may explain everything." He reaches for the door handle and twists.

"The door is locked."

Arsen's dignified demeanor fades as his attempts to force the door fail. The protection charm is proving effective. Arsen sucks in air through his teeth and produces a fake smile.

"Logan, I've traveled a great distance to speak to you and your family. If you'll allow me to—"

Logan shakes his head. "You're not coming in."

Arsen's nostrils flare as he steps away from the front door. He flexes his shoulder and neck muscles, clears his throat, and regains his composure. "Very well. If you insist on making this difficult..."

He straightens the sleeves of his suit as he turns to the side, scanning the neighboring houses. His eyes flick across the street to the nearest house where a little girl sits on the front steps playing with her dolls. With a wicked smirk, Arsen lifts his right hand. In seconds, the five-year-old child floats across the street and into Arsen's arms. The little girl screams at the top of her lungs until her voice is cut off by Arsen's hands forming a ring around her neck.

"Lori!" Logan shouts, opening the door. "Let her go!"

"Invite me in, and sweet Lori can go back home as if this never occurred. She'll remember nothing."

With his hands balled into tight fists, Logan steps out onto the front porch, closing the front door behind him with a click. "I don't know who you are, Arsen. Nor do I care what clan you come from, but Patricia warned us against strangers coming to the house asking to enter."

Ignoring his fuzzy blue house slippers and blue-and-black plaid pajamas, Logan takes another menacing step forward. He feels Patricia's charm pushing into Arsen's aura, forcing Arsen to retreat.

But, aside from Patricia's protective charm, Logan feels something more concrete in his core, in his heart, in the pit of his stomach. In his mind, he sees himself holding a sword and casting spells over mountains lined with soldiers—faded visions that seem like memories. He stands taller, like the man in his vision, and broadens his chest.

With an authority he's never felt before, Logan growls, "Let her go."

A look of utter confusion crosses Arsen's face as he takes another step backward.

"If you don't let her go now, you will die."

The little girl falls limply to the ground as Arsen releases his grip. He swallows hard. "This is certainly an interesting development." He backs away from Logan as casually as possible until his hand reaches his car door. "We'll be in touch soon."

"If I see you again, I will kill you."

After a respectful nod, Arsen slides into his red sports car. He glances back at Logan. "An interesting development indeed, young Logan. Until we meet again."

~ ~ ~

"I don't understand why you have to leave." Kevin loads the last box of Agatha's relics into the back of the truck, right next to the other two boxes and a backpack filled with Logan's clothes and other personal items. "Patricia asked you to send her Nana's relics. You don't have to take them to her personally."

Logan shuts the trunk door and walks to the driver's side.

"I know, Dad, but I want to make sure she gets them."

"But, your mother... I... we need you here." Scratching his head, Kevin looks around the driveway and toward the front yard. "Just send them certified mail."

"Dad, the mail's been a mess since the dragons destroyed the city. Plus, this isn't just any mail. These are Nana's relics. It's important that we make sure Patricia gets them."

"Then I'll take them, and you can stay with your mother."

"No. It has to be me."

"Why?"

"I can't explain why, Dad. Please. Just let me leave. I have to go."

"Logan..." Kevin pauses, stuffs his hands into the side pockets of his blue robe, and shakes his head. He closes his eyes for a second. "I'm so sick and tired of secrets. Please, just tell me what is going on?"

After an exasperated sigh, Logan turns around to look at his father. The sadness in his father's eyes and the dark bags under them stir Logan's chest. "Dad, it's just..."

But, how can he talk to his father about the visceral surges of energy he's felt since early this morning? How does he explain the visions he's had since his confrontation with Arsen— visions of rituals, battles scenes, and men he's never seen before? How can he put into words the primal rage he felt when Arsen took Lori into his hands? How can he explain any of this to his father? His father who is mourning Katarina's death, pained by Jasmyn's estrangement, and coping with his wife's dive into depression.

And how can he explain the story he found in Jasmyn's journal without potentially giving his parents a false sense of hope based on a time-travel spell from one of Nana's stories. It could have been just that, a story and nothing more. Nothing is certain. Regardless, he has to get the journal to Jasmyn and all of Agatha's relics to Patricia. And he needs Patricia to explain what the hell is going on with him.

Logan searches the ground for an excuse to give his father. A perfect lie forms in his mind. Not so much a lie, but a half-truth.

"I... I think I can bring Jaz back home."

"What? How?"

"Yesterday, Brian emailed me saying that she still blames herself for Kat's..."

Although it's been a few days since Katarina's burial, the fact still squeezes his heart. He shifts his balance from one leg to the other as he thinks of another way to say it. There is no other way. He sighs. "For Kat's death."

He stares at the ground for a moment and presses his eyes shut to erase the image of Katarina lying in her coffin. "She blames herself, and I think she believes we blame her too. And, I did, for a little..." Tears well up in his eyes, but he blinks them back. "And she probably knew it. She probably felt it—the way she feels other people's emotions."

"Logan..." His father reaches for Logan's shoulder, but Logan steps back out of reach. "You can't do this to yourself."

"She felt me blame her for Kat's death." He puts his fist against his chest, fighting a grimace. After a deep breath, Logan regains his composure. "She needs to know that I don't blame her. I have to tell her myself. And since the damn phones are still not connecting, I thought I would ask Uncle Gus to take me to the base where she's staying. He'd make sure to bring us back safe and sound."

"Your mother and I should go with you. You're too young to travel by yourself."

"No. I should go alone." Logan blinks rapidly and wipes a single tear at the corner of his eye. "I think I can get through to her."

"Logan—"

"Besides, Mom just took a sedative. She'll be out for hours. She needs you here, with her."

"You can't just leave—"

"Dad!"

Logan steps up close to his father and looks at him with the same authority he felt earlier. "I need to do this. I need to go alone. I'll bring Jaz back. I promise."

Kevin opens his mouth to say something, but then he closes it and nods. After a long, thoughtful gaze into his son's eyes, he lowers his head and stuffs his hands in his robe pockets. "Contact us as soon as you get to Jaz. Don't keep any secrets from us. Okay? And be careful."

Logan embraces his father. "I will."

His father hugs him back with both arms, holding him tight for a few seconds before letting him go. He clears his throat when Logan steps back and away.

With a knot in his throat growing thicker by the second, Logan nods and climbs into the driver's seat. He waves out the window and drives down the road and out of his father's sight.

4

REMEMBERING

A woman in a white truck honks at Logan as he misses the stop sign before entering the ramp to the highway. The blaring sound breaks his daydream. He wrings the steering wheel and attempts to shake the visions invading his mind. The scenes are sharpening as they appear, filling with details that seem too fantastic to be real.

In one vision, two men face each other in a duel that takes place on a foggy edge of a cliff. As they recite poetic spells in another language, a language Logan somehow understands, the men shoot bolts of light from their hands, from the sky, from the ground. They aim them at each other. Rocks crumble down mountainsides as they destroy the earth around them. Thick blankets of fire cover the hillsides, and boulders of ice rain upon the shores.

Logan swerves slightly into the left lane, and the driver of a black SUV honks his horn repeatedly. He regains control of the car and blows a thick burst of air out his mouth. "Concentrate! Get to the airport. Drive. Don't think. Drive."

A serene face fills his mind's eye. Golden wavy hair flows down over her shoulders, and blue eyes shimmer in the sun's rays. Dozens of freckles powder her checks and the bridge of her nose. Her smile radiates joy, and her silky voice calms him. "You are the one, Caderyn. When we marry, our clans will finally be at peace."

Logan shakes his head again. "Concentrate!"

But, the monotonous rhythm of the highway encourages his mind to wander. More battle scenes, more incantations, and a small child reaching up to him for a fatherly embrace. The visions outweigh any attempts Logan makes at focusing on the road. He veers into the left lane once more and another driver blares his horn shouting profanities.

"That's it!"

He pulls over to the highway shoulder, turns off the ignition, takes a deep breath, and closes his eyes.

~ ~ ~

A little girl with auburn hair runs into the arms of a beautiful woman with long blonde locks flowing over her shoulder. She picks the child up in her arms and rocks her side to side.

"Your father is brooding again," the woman teases, her cheek pressed against the child's face.

"Don't play with me, Finna." Caderyn paces with his hands in fists. "I'm in a solemn mood."

"What's happened?"

"The council is in an uproar. Old men bored with a long existence want nothing but conflict. The elders are a curse to our clans."

She kisses the little girl on the forehead. "Go play in your room, Agatha." Once the child leaves, she turns to her husband. "Caderyn, you mustn't upset your council or your elders. My coven worked hard to create an accord. Peace will be dissolved in an instant if you cause a stir."

"The council wants to invalidate our union."

Finna folds her arms across her chest and stares at Caderyn. "On what grounds?"

21

After staring back at his wife for a few seconds, Caderyn looks away and moves to the fireplace. An ominous *thump* echoes in the room with each tired step. The metal pick feels hot in Caderyn's hands as he jabs at the burning pieces of wood. The fire crackles in response.

"They believe you have bewitched me. That you have clouded my judgment and are influencing my decisions. They believe you married me out of false pretenses, for political reasons." He drops the pick and stands to face Finna. "They claim your love is an act and that you have fooled me and the entire clan."

Finna shakes her head. "And what evidence do they hold, or is evidence unnecessary for such claims?"

"The fact that you won't live in the village is one."

She laughs, shaking her head. "I believe living on this peak is a fair compromise considering we are nowhere near my coven's island. I see the horizon and imagine being there, and that's as close as I can get to my home. In the village, I would have no such view. Besides, other families live on the cliff. So, what of it?"

"And, you won't wear the garb of married women of our clan."

Her voice drops an octave. "Because I'm not a woman of your clan."

"I'm merely stating their arguments. Do not lash out at me."

A chilly gust of wind blows in through the window and enrages the fire. Finna rushes over to close the wood shutters. The shawl around her shoulders comes undone and falls to the floor, the white cloth dancing in the last wisps of wind. Caderyn reaches down for the shawl.

"They want me to take action."

22

Finna slips the shawl from Caderyn's hand. "And what action is that?"

"If I nullify our union, they will let us live."

"And if you don't?"

Caderyn glances over at Finna but doesn't say a word.

"My coven will not take this lightly. It will be considered an act of war. Is that what your elders intend? Do they want war?"

"They want what is best for the clan."

"Then have the elders explain their intentions—in front of the council. Accuse *them* of treacherous conduct, of violating their agreement with my coven. A violation which will surely lead to war."

"I have, and the council won't hear it. They demand these conditions."

She presses her lips and frowns. "Then they have agreed to war."

Caderyn removes his thick wool coat and places it on the table, avoiding eye contact with Finna. "I have a few days to think it over before I give them my answer."

"Caderyn, my love, do you need a few days to make your decision?"

"Perhaps, if I nullify the union and send you and Agatha back to your coven—"

"Then you will have dignified their claim."

Caderyn's voice rises into a shout. "At least you will live!"

Finna pauses, brows raised.

He walks to the other side of the room, away from Finna, and leans against the table for support. His head hangs low, and his eyes are shut tight. The low crackling of the fire fills the silence as Caderyn thinks of an alternative.

Finna places her hands upon the back of his shoulders. "You have a strong, loyal following within the clan. Unite several of your brothers, and we'll flee to the Isle of Enid. My coven will offer us protection. And we have many allies."

"You want me to abandon my people?"

"My love," Finna says in a tender tone as she places her arms around his shoulders, "we are on the side of good. We have done nothing but seek peace. Your clan is seeking war. Do you not see the corruption within your council? Please reconsider."

She possesses powers of seduction and persuasion.

That witch wants to control our clan by controlling our leader.

She will deceive you, trick you into abandoning your people.

The elders' claims whisper in Caderyn's mind and fill him with rage. He stands up and shakes Finna's hands off his shoulders. After taking a few steps away, he turns to stare at his wife, the mother of his only child, the love of his life, and possibly the most treacherous of all women he's ever known.

Doubt in his wife grows stronger with each whisper. His bottom lip trembles as he questions her actions, her words, her soft gaze that has him caught in a trance. He pulls himself away from Finna's stare, forcing the whispers back, and storms towards the fire. He grabs the iron pick and pokes the burning lumber once more as he struggles to distinguish accusations from fact, truth from lies.

Finna clears her throat. "It's been a long day, and you have a lot to think about. I'll leave you to your thoughts. Good night... my love." She retreats to her daughter's room and closes the door behind her.

After a long night of restless sleep, filled with hellish nightmares, Caderyn awakens to the midday sun. A light sandalwood scent floats upwards from ashes burning next to his side of the bed. He waves the smoke away with his hand and sits up, unable to recall when he lit the sleep-inducing incense.

"Finna?"

He scans the room and rises to his feet.

"Finna!" he calls out across the house.

No one replies.

As he searches the house, he finds several unloaded cases of clothing in their changing room, open drawers emptied out in a hurry, blankets and clothing on his daughter's bed, and Agatha's most precious doll splayed out on the floor. Dread fills his heart with every step he takes in the empty house.

He looks out the window toward the Isle of Enid, and although his heart is aching from her desertion, he understands her rationale—she is protecting her daughter. He would have done the same if he were in her shoes.

But then, he hears the elders' words in his mind.

The witches have always hated us.

They only want our power.

Finna is the most devious of them all.

She will steal everything from you. She will take your soul.

"No," Caderyn says weakly, and turns toward the locked treasure room.

The door is ajar.

He rushes inside the room and opens the trunk that holds his family's most valuable possession. He falls back on his knees, his shoulders in a slump and his mouth agape. The ancient dragon eggs that have been passed down his family line for generations are missing.

The elders' accusations were true.

Within seconds, hatred and rage mixed with the pain of

25

utter betrayal consume his heart. Caderyn lifts the trunk and slams it against the back wall. One by one, he takes every item in his home and smashes it on the ground, growling with each crash.

How could you do this to me, Finna?

An intricate wooden carving of them from their union ceremony, created by Caderyn's brother, splinters into pieces when Caderyn flings it against the wall.

All of it, every single piece of our home, every single day in our life together, it was all a lie!

Figurines of good fortune that were given to them by friends and families upon their daughter's birth, glass vases holding trinkets of family jewelry, and other keepsakes from their home shatter against the wooden floors. Caderyn destroys every single memory of their life together, of their false union, of their pretend happiness.

He storms outside and stares back at the home he and Finna created. The bushes Finna planted years ago, full of bright red and purple roses, mock him. The cherry blossom trees lining the border of his side garden release hundreds of tiny white petals, falling like confetti in celebration of her successful treason. Even the pure white curtains peeking through Agatha's bedroom window are evidence of the extent of Finna's treachery.

You will pay, Finna. Your coven will pay for your deception!

Caderyn releases one final roar before burning their home to ground.

5

OLD FRIENDS

The betrayal Caderyn felt in that memory burrows inside Logan's chest. He grasps at his heart, pushing inward with his fist, pressing his ribcage as if it will keep his chest from bursting. He can't inhale, caught in a whirlwind of confusion and agony.

When the vision dissipates, Logan gasps for air as if he's just finished a sprint. He pulls out his phone to call his uncle but finds there is still no service. He slams the phone into the passenger seat where it bounces and then tumbles to the passenger side floor.

Logan leans back in his seat, lowers his hands weakly onto his lap, and stares out over the dashboard into the distance.

"I'm going crazy. I must be going crazy. No. This is no hallucination. This is something else."

His gaze hops around from cloud to cloud, bush to bush, looking for something to focus on, something real.

No. I'm not going crazy. These are not hallucinations. These, these... visions are about Finna, Nana's mother... and Caderyn? Finna and Caderyn... why am I getting these visions? They feel real, like they're my own memories. How can I possibly have memories of people I've never met?

Logan jolts to alertness. Something near him, behind him, sends waves of gentle electricity up against his back. His skin hairs stand upright, and a chill passes through his entire body.

When he turns around to look out the rear window, he

spots the red sports car parked several yards behind him on the side road, the same sports car in which Arsen drove away. With rage building inside, Logan curls his upper lip and steps out of his car.

The vibrations emanating from Arsen push against his torso, demanding to be felt, to be surrendered to, but Logan shoves them back. With every step toward Arsen, Logan rolls his hands into tight fists and then stretches his fingers outwards into a claw. He rolls his shoulders forward and turns his head side to side. Logan flexes and contracts all the muscles in his hands, neck, arms, and shoulders until he reaches Arsen.

"Get out of the car!" Logan bares his teeth, ready to fight. "Now!"

Arsen presses his lips as he opens the door. He steps out of the driver's seat with his arms raised in the air, palms facing forward. "There is no need to be upset with me. I'm not causing those visions."

"How do you know about that?"

Arsen's lips give a hint of a smile. "Reading your thoughts is one of my many talents."

A gust of wind passes between them as another vision forces its way into Logan's mind. He presses his eyes tight and rubs his temples as a slight headache ensues, and the images clarify.

"There's no fighting it," Arsen says.

Logan sits down on a nearby rock and peers up at Arsen from under his eyebrows.

"You're going to have to just accept it."

~ ~ ~

In front of the council stands a rickety mess of an old

man, barely able to walk, his bones about to collapse from the weight of his skin. Yet, his voice is resonant as he shouts at Caderyn. "You owe it to your people, to our clansmen, to find that witch and kill her."

Another elder points his disjointed, wrinkly finger at Caderyn. "You have wasted your efforts these past years on conquering other lands and peoples, and yet that traitor still lives."

Caderyn sits at the front of the grand assembly room in his designated chair facing all the men of the council. "Is it not so easy as you say, Jal. You and Oric are too eager to start a fight."

"Has she still a hold on you, Caderyn? Are you still bewitched?" Oric shouts outward for all to hear, finishing with a cough as he sits back down.

As the grand council dissolves into mumbles and grunting conversations, Caderyn glares at the two cursed elders, both withering away from centuries of bitter existence. Although their accusations anger him, Caderyn revels in the fact that not all elders are gifted with everlasting youth. He smirks complacently in their direction.

Another elder, who has the appearance of a young man in his thirties even though he is centuries old, stands and raises his hands to calm the arguments among the council members. "My brothers, you know very well that Caderyn is an astute leader. He knows what is right and what must be done."

"Ryland," Caderyn's booming voice addresses the speaker. "What is your advice upon this matter?"

The wooden chairs in the great hall all shuffle as the elders turn to face Ryland. Not a single sound is heard as everyone awaits a response.

"My advice is to gather our men, all of our forces, and

attack Finna and her coven once and for all."

A wave of mumbles fills the great hall, and Ryland raises his hands to calm it once more.

"Rid us of this enemy, including the child. Then we can once again concentrate on the greatness of the Foreman Clan. We have spent too many years upon this matter. It is time to end it."

"That is my child you speak of."

"You see!" Oric stands, pointing his decrepit finger at Caderyn. "He is still under her enchantment." He turns to the crowd. "How do we even know it is your child?"

A tumultuous grumble fills the room as council members rise from their seats and raise their hands in protest. Some in defense of Caderyn, most of them attacking.

Ryland raises his hands and begs the council to resume order. "My brothers, you all know that I can see the truth before me. The visions have been clear on this matter."

The men halt their protests and take their seats. Once silence has returned, Ryland continues.

"Agatha is, in fact, Caderyn's child. However, she is not his heir. She is Finna's heir. She is part of Finna's coven, and that makes her our enemy."

Every single member of the council nods.

"So," Ryland continues, "I look to you, Caderyn, the strongest leader this clan has ever known, to consider the greatness of the Foreman Clan, your brethren, before the survival of our enemy."

~ ~ ~

Arsen yells Logan's name three times before finally pulling him out of his trance.

Logan grabs the shirt at Arsen's chest and lifts him off the ground. "What are you doing to me?"

"I'm not doing anything. These visions are part of the transfer of power between you and Caderyn."

He shoves Arsen back several steps. "The transfer of power?"

"Yes. It seems you are chosen to inherit his powers. The transfer of magic has begun."

The words echo in Logan's ears as his mind is carried away to Caderyn's transfer ceremony. He finds the rock and sits back down, allowing the memory to flow in.

~ ~ ~

Centuries ago, in the center of a thick forest clearing, Caderyn stands before his father. Select clansmen watch silently, acting as witnesses, as Caderyn's father recites the spell. "My time is come. Step forward, my son."

Although Caderyn knows the details of the ritual, his arms tremble with nerves. He flexes his shoulder and neck muscles and steps closer to his father.

With a sigh of satisfaction, his father wipes the blade with his tunic. "Are you ready, Caderyn?"

Caderyn nods, clears the knot in his throat, and blinks rapidly to keep the tears at bay. His father hands him the blade, steps back, widening his stance, and gives Caderyn a long nod.

Thrusting forward, Caderyn jams the sharp blade easily into his father's stomach. His father accepts the strike with a low grunt followed by a long, trembling sigh.

Caderyn leans into his father's chest as he pulls the knife out and flings it into the dirt floor. The other clansmen surround their dying leader as Caderyn lays his father flat on the ground.

He takes his father's right hand into his, gripping it tightly, and returns his intense stare, a mixture of tranquility and sorrow. He bends down closer as his father speaks his final words.

"Do not... fail... our people."

~ ~ ~

The heartache Caderyn felt at that moment passes now through Logan's heart, and a feeling of pride rises in his chest. Logan lifts his eyes to meet Arsen's stare. "You were there."

Arsen nods. "I was."

The knowledge of his ancestry settles in Logan's mind. The dirt shoulder of the highway acts as a canvas for the visions trickling into his memory. Political struggles with immortal elders and council members, mistrust among the clan leaders, falling in love with Finna, the betrayal that followed, the declaration of war against her coven, and the decades of battles that ended with the dragons virtually eliminating their clan's existence.

Graphic battle scenes burrow into permanent spots in Logan's mind—dead women and children, dragon carcasses, destroyed villages, and the burning remains of his clansmen. The rush of memories and emotions, the conflicting feelings of anger and affinity toward his brothers, and the vibrations stemming from Arsen's direction all make Logan feel nauseated.

Logan steps toward his truck, wobbling as the dizziness takes hold, and he falls to his hands and knees. He heaves several times before throwing up.

Arsen places one hand on Logan's back. "You are Caderyn's next of kin and heir. You are part of our clan now."

Logan stands back up and wipes his mouth clean of vomit. "I will never be one of you." He staggers backward. "You waged war against my grandmother's coven."

Arsen tilts his head. "Do you not recall the deception? Finna, Agatha's mother, used Caderyn and betrayed him and all of us. We all trusted and believed in her. We were all bewitched."

Shaking his head, Logan tries to make sense of his visions, Arsen's arguments, and the little Patricia has told him of the fight against the Foreman Clan. "I have to get to Jasmyn," he mumbles and walks back to his truck.

"I don't think you understand. I can't simply let you go. You're Caderyn's heir, and although I haven't confirmed his intentions yet, I'm assuming he would want me to lead you back to him."

Logan stops at the driver's side door. He turns on his toes. "Why? So, I can kill him and take over the clan?"

"Perhaps, if he wishes. It's what he did with his father. It is the way of our people."

"I'm not one of you!"

"Whether you like it or not, Logan, you are."

Logan glares at Arsen for a brief moment before opening the side door and climbing in.

"Logan, will you just—"

"My sister, my family, comes first, before you or Caderyn or your clan!"

"Then for your sister's sake—"

Logan turns on the ignition and stomps the accelerator. The engine muffles Arsen's voice. The truck's wheels screech along the pavement as Logan peels off onto the road.

6

THE CHASE

Going back to work after Katarina's funeral has not been easy for Gustavo. The image of his eight-year-old niece lying in the small casket still haunts him. He failed his sister, Paula, when he promised he would return from the chaos with all three of her children safe and sound. He failed to protect his niece, and he has to live with it.

Watching his sister go insane with grief and his brother-in-law tending to her madness was more than he could bear. It's only been a few days since the funeral, but Gustavo was eager to get back to work, hoping that the persistent images from the funeral would dissipate with his daily tasks. But as soon as he walked in today, Gustavo was bombarded by coworkers offering their condolences and asking about the state of the family.

It's been a heavy morning.

After several conversations, Gustavo needs a break, some fresh air. He walks out the front entrance of the hangar and sits down on an iron bench bolted to the concrete. Spreading his arms out along the back of the bench, Gustavo inhales deeply and exhales. The spring air filling his lungs has a therapeutic effect on his mind. He closes his eyes and accepts the sunlight warming his body. For a moment, he feels positive that the worst has passed, and it is now time to heal.

The sound of an approaching vehicle breaks his meditation. When he opens his eyes, he sees a truck drive up to the parking station in front of him. He cocks his head when he recognizes Logan behind the steering wheel, and he stands to meet him halfway. Gustavo notices the anxious look on Logan's face as he jumps out of the driver's side, and a knot forms in the pit of his stomach. His heart beats faster, but he remains calm—years of working in the military and emergency services is serving him well.

"Logan, what are you doing here?"

"Can you fly me to Patricia and Jasmyn?"

"Why?"

Logan peeks over his shoulder and then makes a full circle, scanning the area, before facing Gustavo. "Patricia asked for all of Nana's relics."

"I can get Walter to fly us, but… calm down. Why are you so tense? Did something happen with your parents?"

"No, they're fine."

"Do they know you're here?"

"Mom is taking sedatives, and Dad knows. But…"

Gustavo watches patiently as Logan runs his fingers through his hair, pacing back and forth between the truck and the iron bench. Logan cracks his knuckles and then stretches out his fingers before rubbing them together. He shakes his shoulders and tilts his head side to side, flexing his back and shoulder muscles, before stopping in front of Gustavo.

"Remember that story Patricia told us, about the dragons defeating the Foreman Clan?"

"Yeah. What about it?"

"A guy from that clan is following me."

Gustavo looks down the road behind Logan's truck. "The Foreman Clan? Are you sure?"

Logan nods. "That's what he said."

"What's he driving?"

"A red European sports car, like a Lamborghini or a

Porsche. He's got blonde hair and is wearing a gray suit."

"Hold on."

Gustavo pulls his military radio from its clip on his belt. He asks someone on the radio if they've seen a man in a gray suit driving a red European sports car in their vicinity.

"This guy's not exactly incognito," a guy responds on the radio after a minute. "Gray suit, slick blonde hair, sunglasses, red Maserati. He's on camera eleven, parked along the road leading to your hangar, just behind the bend. You probably can't see him. Do you want me to send security?"

"Yes. He might be armed, so be careful." Gustavo places the radio back on his belt clip and turns to Logan. "Let's get this stuff to Patricia. Now, tell me everything that happened at the house."

"Okay." Logan sighs as they walk toward the hangar's entrance. "This is how it all went down…"

~ ~ ~

With the engine off and the windows rolled down, Arsen sits in his car and contemplates his next move. While reading Logan's thoughts earlier, he learned of Logan's plan to take Agatha's relics to Patricia. He recalls Patricia's face from Logan's thoughts and sighs.

Those wondrous eyes.

The temptation to follow him to Patricia conflicts with Caderyn's orders to gather Agatha's relics and return home. But, when he saw Caderyn last night, he wasn't undergoing the transfer. The situation has changed, and the consequences of his next move are drastically more severe than before.

He pulls his phone out of his suit's inner pocket, recalling that data service is available at the airport. He stares at the phone and is about to select Caderyn's number to send him a message when Patricia's face appears in his mind. His fingers tingle at the possibility of seeing her again, and his heart races as he imagines all the possible outcomes to their meeting. He slips the phone back into his suit pocket and decides to follow Logan.

The sound of a car's brakes draws Arsen's attention. In the rear-view mirror, he sees an officer step out of his vehicle and walk up to the driver's side window.

"Good afternoon officer." Arsen smiles. "What seems to be the problem?"

The young officer stands two feet away from the driver's door, with his right hand resting on his pistol's holster and the other hand on his club. He asks Arsen to step out of the car. When Arsen doesn't open the door, he repeats his command in a harsher tone, stepping back from the vehicle. He unlatches the gun holster on his belt and glances at the second security car that accompanied him to the scene. The lights flash.

While staring at the officer's sunglasses, Arsen whispers a spell. A slight grin appears on Arsen's face as he utters the last word.

The officer's shoulders relax, and he stands up straight. He lowers his hands from his holster and waves at the second car to turn off the emergency lights. The officer tips his hat and smiles at Arsen. "Have a good day, sir."

"Thank you, officer. And don't forget to tell your superiors that I left without any issues."

"Yes, sir." The officer walks back to his car and drives away, the second car following his lead.

With a smug smirk on his face, Arsen drives on toward the hangar.

As he parks his car, a helicopter lifts off, and he knows Logan is on board. He walks straight into the building, and within minutes a crew is preparing a helicopter for immediate departure.

~ ~ ~

When Regina woke yesterday morning to the news of Katarina's death, Regina mourned in a way she never had before. Not even when her mother or sisters died did her chest ache with such pain that breathing took considerable effort. She couldn't believe Katarina, the tiniest of her coven members, only eight years old, was gone. She recited multiple prayers all day long, over and over, crying uncontrollably. She fell asleep in the evening when her body was unable to withstand the suffering any longer.

After a dreamless, recuperating sleep, Regina wakes with a less piercing ache in her heart.

"Time to get up." Patricia shakes Regina's foot when she walks into the hospital room. She opens the window shades to allow the morning light in.

"I don't want to get up." Regina covers her head with her blanket.

Patricia whips the blanket off and moves the cart with a breakfast tray closer to the bed. "I have mourned enough for the both of us. Now you have to heal. Jasmyn needs us."

The morning activities at the NAS Fallon military hospital commence quickly—nurse examinations, muscle massages, and physical therapy. The therapist finishes her session with one last leg exercise to stimulate blood circulation in Regina's legs. The lunch tray comes rolling in as soon as the physical therapist leaves the room, and Regina's stomach grumbles.

After swallowing a bite of the hospital-cooked chicken

meal, Regina purses her lips. A long gulp of bottled water washes away the dry, flavorless taste. She places a soggy piece of broccoli in her mouth but then spits it out. She pushes the food tray away.

"Lunch here sucks. Breakfast was better."

"You can't have everything."

As the taste dissipates, Regina shakes her head. "I still can't believe Katarina had to die for Jasmyn to execute the spell. Poor Jasmyn, she must be devastated."

Patricia nods. "There's no doubt she's still suffering. She tries to hide it from us, but we can all see it."

"Poor kid. Maybe you shouldn't leave her alone. Where is she now?"

"She's with Brian. She went with him to practice some elemental spells in the desert early this morning. They might be back at the apartment by now. The exercise is good for her; it will get her mind off of things. Maybe she'll find atonement by learning the magic."

"Well, at least she's out in the fresh spring air. Nature has a way of healing such injuries."

"I hope so. Maybe it'll give her some peace."

A handsome, young orderly in a blue uniform comes into the room and empties out the garbage bins. Regina straightens her back when she notices the definition in his biceps and the squareness of his jawline. She watches intently as he changes the sheets of the bed next to hers. Once he finishes collecting the sheets into a plastic bag, Regina thanks him and smiles coyly. When the orderly leaves the room, Regina sighs.

Patricia rolls her eyes to the side.

"What?" She shoots back at Patricia. "I like to admire beauty, and *that* was beautiful. Speaking of which... Brian seems like quite the match for Jasmyn."

"In her state, I doubt she's even thinking about that. But, he definitely has a positive effect on her. When he's near, her aura brightens just a bit, turns a bit blue even, but then it grays out again."

"She's punishing herself." Regina slides to the edge of the hospital bed. "We've all gone through that phase. Surviving our loved ones is never easy, especially when we survive our younger siblings. We've all watched our baby brothers and sisters die."

Patricia walks over to help Regina stand up. "Yes, but we've never felt responsible for their deaths."

After lifting Regina to her feet, Patricia attempts a spell to help reverse the muscle atrophy in her legs, but it fails. The physical cost of executing spells against magical beings like the Gregorn Dragons was more than Regina's body could withstand.

"Oh give it up, Patricia. You know you suck at healing. That's my gift. You're the bruiser, and I'm the healer."

"Not much good those restoration powers are doing now."

"It's not my fault I can't heal myself. I don't make the rules."

With Regina's arm around her shoulders, Patricia helps her sister take a walk around the hospital floor.

"Come on, Regina. Pick up your feet."

"I am!"

"It doesn't feel like you are."

Patricia glances up just in time to see a young soldier in a brown uniform smiling at Regina. Regina returns an even brighter smile and stands upright for a split second, straightening her back and chest, before her legs give out and she's leaning her weight on Patricia once more.

Patricia rolls her eyes. "If you don't try harder, I'm

letting you fall. Flirting from the hospital floor isn't sexy."

"I *am* trying. This isn't easy." As they reach the end of the hallway, Regina hears a faint ringing emanating from her room. "I think someone is calling you."

Patricia grunts as she turns Regina around to walk back. "It's going to have to wait."

7

CLANSMEN

The evergreen trees surrounding the clearing shuffle together against the windstorm, protecting the camp from the arctic breeze. Auroras paint the night sky in streaks of blue and pink hues as Caderyn sits with his father in front of the campfire the night before their transfer ceremony.

"Son," Caderyn's father says as he tosses several twigs into the fire pit, "don't wait too long to marry and have an heir."

Caderyn picks up his own set of twigs and flips them into the fire. "Why? You waited centuries before starting a family."

"Yes, but I don't have the benefit of vague memories. The details of my past are vivid and unforgiving, and not as glorious as I had hoped. I've had many triumphs, but more sorrow than I care to recall, and the sorrowful memories always have the most clarity. Live a short and happy life, instead of a long and trivial one."

Caderyn cocks his head at his father's statement. "But, you've lived a great life. I've already inherited many of your memories, and I don't see anything to regret."

"Once you inherit all my memories, you'll understand my meaning."

"What will I see that I don't already know? You have three daughters and a son, a family who loves you. The clansmen would follow you to the ends of the world if you would lead the way. Our people are united and stronger than ever. What is there to know?"

His father searches the ground and picks up a long wiry branch. He sighs and meets Caderyn's eager stare. "You will learn that you, your existence, has been my only peace in this world."

"Peace from what?"

His father jabs at the fire with the branch and flames whip up into the night, dancing in the air for a moment before disappearing as if they never existed. "When I married your mother, I did not love her."

Caderyn shakes his head. "I know it was an arranged marriage, but it's worked out, has it not? Love is not the only requirement for a successful marriage. And you had children, a large family, a good home—every man's wish. Do you regret all of this?"

"I don't regret marrying your mother. It gave me all that and more. But long before I met your mother, centuries before, I loved another woman. Truly loved her. And, I chose *not* to be with her."

The fire crackles again as Caderyn stares intently at his father, waiting patiently for him to continue.

"She wanted to marry and have children right away. A male heir could potentially lead to the end of my immortality, the end of my power over the clan. I was young, and I wasn't ready to give it all up. So, I chose *not* to marry her. I chose power and immortality."

After a long silence, Caderyn asks, "What happened to her?"

His father lowers his gaze and releases the heavy sigh of a man who has lived a long, tough life. "A few years later, she married another, had many children, and died an old woman surrounded by dozens of grandchildren. She lived a short, simple, happy life."

He rests his elbows on his knees and looks up at Caderyn with an apologetic stare. "After she died, I was overcome with immense grief. I mourned for decades. I regretted leaving her. I regretted choosing my position over her. Centuries passed, and I still suffered—until I had you. Your sisters soon followed, and I found a sense of peace with my children."

Caderyn leans back on the rock he sits upon and shrugs his shoulders. "Then you and she both lived well. You both had good lives."

"The goal is to live a life without regret, or with as few regrets as possible. Because, no matter how much time passes, regrets never seems to go away, especially those that cannot be undone. It's like a shadow—it appears strongest when there is brightness in your world. When I had you, it was the happiest day of my life, and at the same time I was struck with grief."

"Grief?" Caderyn cocks his head back. "But why?"

His father glances down at his hands folded in front of him. "You were the son I was meant to have with her. You were the son she wanted, with me, but I chose otherwise. Not a day goes by that I don't regret my decision." He chuckles sadly and shakes his head. "Even now, as I gaze upon the end of my life, I'm unable to reflect upon anything else other than my regret."

After staring at the ground and recalling wonderful moments with his mother and father, along with his sisters, Caderyn lifts his gaze at his father. "Did you ever love my mother?"

"Of course I loved your mother—I learned to love her. There are many forms of love, as you will learn. But, the kind of love I had so long ago..." He leans forward onto one knee and presses his fist against his chest, staring intensely at Caderyn. "If you are lucky enough to obtain it, you must never let it go."

~ ~ ~

Once the flight to Manchester reaches cruising altitude, a flight attendant in a green suit hands Kean and Caderyn a steaming white towel. She pulls a small notepad from her front pocket and clicks a pen in her right hand.

"On the menu today, we have grilled sirloin, roasted chicken breast, or parmesan-crusted salmon with your choice of steamed vegetables, sweet potato fries, or quinoa rice mix with pecans and cranberries. A house salad is optional, and we have a variety of dressings."

Kean glances at the bottom hemline of the flight attendant's short skirt. "I'll have the grilled sirloin, medium rare, more bloody than not. The quinoa rice, and a house salad with vinaigrette dressing."

"And to drink?"

He rolls his gaze up to meet hers, and his lips turn upward into a half-smile. "Red wine, of course."

"Very good." She returns a flirtatious smile, then turns to Caderyn. "And for you, sir?"

Kean nudges Caderyn out of his trance. "Your dinner order?"

He glares at Kean and then turns to the flight attendant. "Salmon, vegetables, and white wine. No salad."

"Very good. I'll be back shortly with your drinks."

When the flight attendant leaves, Caderyn returns his gaze to the seat in front of him.

I saw your pain that night, Father, and the next day I felt it in my heart. I took your advice and married Finna as soon as I could, but what good did it bring me? Of all the lessons I've learned from you, nothing prepared me for Finna's betrayal. It tore me apart. It destroyed my clan. Trust. Honor. Loyalty. Our clan stood upon those pillars once. But when the pillars broke… Now, what course of action do you suggest I take, Father? The transfer has begun, and I sit next to a brother who will kill me the instant he learns of it. Trust, honor, loyalty…

Caderyn huffs.

Kean leans in. "You seem out of sorts, brother. Is something the matter?"

"If I seem preoccupied, it's because I'm planning our contingency. If Arsen returns without a dragon egg, then we will have to focus our efforts on the girl and the relic holding the red dragon. It will be difficult to persuade her to release it, so I have asked Ryland to investigate further. But in case Ryland comes up short, we will need an alternate plan. There is much to think about."

After a few moments, Kean pulls out his phone and taps on the screen. "Have you seen Agatha's grandchildren?"

"I have."

"Isn't it interesting how similar the girl is to Agatha? Her name is Jasmyn; she's practically her twin. And her brother, Logan, looks remarkably like you when you were young. Have you seen him close up? Here's a photo of—"

"I'm not interested in gawking at Agatha's relations. I've seen enough of them. We need to focus on our plan."

"Forgive me." Kean lowers his eyes. "I'm a victim of my own astonishment. I'll say nothing more about the girl or her brother."

As Kean speaks to another flight attendant walking by, Caderyn wipes the side of his head just above his right ear where a few tiny beads of sweat have collected. He feels his energy draining, a force pulling invisible strands of muscle tissue from his arms, legs, and torso, up and outward away from his being.

With the same calculated movement, he wipes the other side of his head, making sure that Kean is unaware of his actions or his current state.

Caderyn raises his head high and holds it firm as if nothing is the matter. But, he knows the source of his weakness. The moment he caught a glimpse of Logan's face on the news earlier that morning, Caderyn felt the jolt. He knew instantly his clan's magic chose Logan to inherit his powers. His time has come, and he must be careful.

Just breathe. There can be no signs of weakness. None.

~ ~ ~

Logan and Gustavo arrive at NAS Fallon and head straight to the hospital. When Gustavo walks into Regina's hospital room, Patricia smiles at the rush of happiness at seeing him. But when Logan walks into the room a few seconds later, her smile diminishes from the shock of his strong, commanding aura. Fixing him with a careful expression, she asks, "What's going on? Is everyone okay?"

Without hesitation, Logan summarizes the events of the morning. Patricia quietly gasps when Logan mentions Arsen's name, and swallows hard when he mentions Caderyn's.

"Caderyn is supposed to be dead," Regina says. "Agatha killed him."

"Not according to Arsen," Logan says.

With her eyes narrowed, Patricia steps around Regina's bed and closes the space between Logan and herself. When she feels the shield surrounding Logan's body, she stops her approach. She curses under her breath and shakes her head.

"Did you tell your uncle about what you've been going through?"

Cheeks flushing, Logan glances at Gustavo and then back at Patricia. "I didn't. I just—"

"What's going on?" Gustavo asks. He steps in front of his nephew. "Logan, look what keeping secrets has done to our family." Gustavo gives Logan a stern look. "Tell me what's going on."

Pressing his lips into a tight line, Logan looks to the side and nods. He maintains eye contact with the floor as he explains his visions—the anguish he felt when Caderyn stabbed his father to complete the transfer, battle scenes with his clan brothers on distant lands, and the anger and rage that engulfed him when he experienced Finna's betrayal.

He describes details down to the hilt of the blade Caderyn's father gave him on the evening before the transfer ceremony, and the sleeping gown Finna was wearing the night before she ran away with their daughter. Logan's words flow out of his mouth like a high waterfall trickling down a smooth mountainside, mesmerizing everyone.

"And the worst part is," Logan says, his eyes widening, "After I saw the visions, I didn't want to hurt Arsen anymore. I felt… close to him. Like we were brothers, somehow." He shakes his head. "The idea that I can feel close to Arsen and at the same time hate him, knowing that he and his clan tried to kill Nana and Patricia and…" Logan crosses his arms again and finally raises his eyes to look at Patricia. His stare pleads for help, guidance, a plan of some sort.

Instead, he meets Patricia's scowl.

"Patricia," Regina whispers harshly from her hospital bed. "It's not his fault."

"Are you so quick to forgive them too?"

"Hey, I have all of my mother's memories too, you know. I remember everything the Foreman Clan did to us. I'm not forgiving anyone. But Logan is innocent."

"Caderyn is sharing his memories and emotions. He already considers Arsen a brother. I can feel his aura forcing me away!" She rubs her temples with the tips of her fingers and takes a deep breath. "He'll get sucked into their clan and turn against us, just like Caderyn did."

"You don't know that."

"What do you think will happen, Regina? Do you honestly believe, after all that we've been through with the Foreman Clan, that they'll let Logan make peace with us? He's their leader."

"Not yet. He has to kill Caderyn to complete the transfer."

"It doesn't matter. They don't want peace. They've never wanted peace. They've only ever wanted war. Finna married Caderyn and had a child with him, for goodness sake. If that wasn't enough to make them want peace, then nothing will!"

Crossing her arms tightly across her chest, Patricia walks over to the window and stares out at the clouds stretching across the midday sky, searching for a way to keep these forces of magic from controlling Jasmyn and Logan's lives.

"What if I don't want to be the clan's new leader?" Logan asks.

"It's not up to you, darling." Regina looks at Logan with apologetic eyes. "Caderyn only needs to acknowledge you as his kin, his heir, for a split second, and then his clan's magic decides if you are to be his chosen one. The transfer starts immediately, whether you or Caderyn want it to or not. And it completes when you kill him." Regina sits back and rubs her forehead.

"What happens if I don't kill Caderyn?"

Regina and Patricia glance at each other. Neither answer Logan's question.

After a few seconds of tense silence, Logan trembles, as if something physically shocked him. He walks around Regina's bed to the window and looks outside.

"What is it?" Patricia asks.

He walks to the hospital room's door, looks down the hall both ways, then walks back into the room. "He's here. Arsen. Nearby. Maybe downstairs, by the entrance. He said he was after Nana's things."

"Where are the relics?"

Gustavo steps forward. "In the car, downstairs."

"He could have easily taken them by now." She paces alongside the hospital bed with her hands on her hips. "No, he's here for something else."

"Or someone else." Gustavo glances at Logan before looking back at Patricia.

Patricia shakes her head. "That's not happening." She marches around the bed. "Everyone stay here. I'm going to have a word with Arsen."

Once Patricia reaches the door, she pauses and then turns around. "Oh, and Logan, can I ask you to please do me a favor?"

Logan looks up at Patricia with eager, hopeful eyes. His aura drops its guard. "Anything."

She whispers a spell, and Logan falls unconscious on the hospital bed.

"What the hell did you do?" Gustavo shouts, grabbing Logan's sleeping body before it slides to the floor.

"Arsen and I have some unresolved issues. If our meeting goes sour, Logan might feel compelled to help his clan brother, and I don't want to have to hurt him."

Gustavo glares at Patricia.

"Remember, the Foreman Clan is still our enemy."

8

ANCIENT RIVALS

"Well, I must say, you're a sight for these tired old eyes."

With a winning smile stretching from ear to ear, and his arms swinging casually back and forth, Arsen strolls across the hospital lobby toward Patricia. He notices a hint of a smile on her face, and his skin tingles.

"You look anything but tired."

"And you look as lovely as ever." He reaches out his hand for hers and raises her hand to his lips to plant a gentle kiss.

Her smile diminishes. "What do you want, Arsen?"

"The chance to see you again presented itself. I'd have been a fool not to take it."

"I know you're not here to see me. Logan's told us everything."

With narrowed eyes, Arsen concentrates on reading Patricia's mind, but to no avail. "It's always refreshing speaking to someone with a shielded aura. You seldom find people with such a gift."

Patricia rolls her eyes and glances to the side.

"Mortals often act contrary to their true intentions. Although reading their deepest thoughts gives me insight, it makes for a rather boring interaction. I know all the cards they're holding—what fun is that? You, however, are a riddle, and I find that," he sighs, "invigorating."

"Why are you following Logan?" Her voice rings

harsher than before.

Arsen lessens his smile and lowers his gaze to the ground. "Do you ever wonder," he looks back up at Patricia from under his eyebrows, "how different our lives would've been if Finna hadn't betrayed Caderyn? We might still be together. You would still love me as you once did. Maybe we'd have children of our own."

"I doubt you lack children in this world."

He smirks. "You are correct on that account. I've had children; some have died of old age, some are still alive. All are unaware of my existence. They were born out of solitary moments of lust from mothers who'd forgotten my name by the next morning. No, our child would've been different."

Patricia crosses her arms. "Why are you here?"

"Answer me honestly, and I'll tell you everything you want you know. Do you ever wonder?"

"And then you'll tell me everything?"

"Everything."

"Fine."

She takes a long, deep breath.

"I suppose we would have remained together, had several children, grown old and achy, and lived our last days staring out into the sunset, as we used to talk about when we were young. That could have been our fate—if only Caderyn hadn't taken advice from a war-hungry council."

Arsen purses his lips and lowers his gaze.

"Even after they annulled the marriage, after some time of relative peace between our peoples, we could have reunited and lived happily ever after, to some degree. But, we didn't have peace, did we? Instead, Caderyn and your council waged decades of war against us, seeking revenge on Finna whose only true crime was saving her child from your clan's wrath. Your men killed my sisters and their families in their sleep; you murdered children too helpless to defend themselves. And, as a result, we were forced to create the Gregorn Dragons to protect ourselves from you."

"And they annihilated us," Arsen says sharply.

"Yes, *that* they did. And even after the wars were over, after the dragons reduced your clan to nothing, perhaps if you had come begging on your hands and knees for forgiveness, just maybe I would have found an ounce of mercy in my heart to forgive you. But that didn't happen, did it? No. And we didn't have peace, did we?"

He lifts his eyes to meet her stare.

"Did we?"

"No, you didn't."

"The dragons rebelled and obliterated my coven."

Arsen lowers his gaze once more.

"You, Arsen, were one of Caderyn's most trusted brothers, friends since your infancy, possibly the most influential of them all. Regardless of your love for me or any consideration you might have had for my sisters, you did nothing to dissuade him. You chose to play your council's destructive game, which destroyed all of us."

Patricia steps closer without breaking her stare.

"So, to answer your question, Arsen... yes, I've wondered how different our lives would've been if you had acted differently. But, I stopped wondering long ago, and I don't waste my time with such trivialities. Things are as they are, and what was done can never be undone."

Arsen stands with one hand clasping his other wrist behind his back. He frowns and nods. "That was an eloquent speech. There's no doubt you've given the question much thought."

"If you are quite through reviewing our past and pretending there is a potential for an alternate universe, tell me why you are following Logan. He has already told us about Caderyn, and we know he is going through the transfer."

"Then you understand he is one of us."

Patricia inhales and purses her lips. "What is Caderyn's plan? What does he intend to do with Logan?"

"I'm not aware of Caderyn's plans with regard to Logan."

Lifting her right hand as if holding a small bowl full of water, Patricia executes a spell that brings Arsen to his knees. "You're testing my patience."

He chuckles and then groans as the wrap around his torso squeezes inward. "If this is as close as I can get to you…"

The tips of her fingers curl inward, and Arsen groans louder.

"My orders, as of yesterday when I last spoke to Caderyn…" Arsen grunts and tries to stand to his feet, "were to go to Agatha's home and gather all her relics." He coughs deeply and gasps. "He wants the entrapment case holding the red dragon… and any dragon eggs left. That's all. He said nothing… about Logan."

"I don't believe you."

He chuckles weakly. "You must think so little of me." He grunts again. "If I wanted to take Logan, I would have done it before he reached you. I had plenty of opportunities."

She lessens the invisible blanket's hold to allow Arsen to speak.

He coughs and clears his throat as he pushes himself to his feet. "Caderyn was not undergoing the transfer when I last saw him. It must have started earlier this morning. I haven't spoken to him since last night."

"Why not?"

As he straightens his back and lifts his head high, he looks deep into Patricia's eyes. "I saw you in Logan's thoughts. I knew he intended to contact you about our meeting." A weak smile flickers across Arsen's face.

She shakes her head.

"Is it so unbelievable that I would want to see you again?"

Against her will, Patricia's mind floods with a distant memory of a teenage Arsen chasing her up a daisy-filled hillside in the middle of a cloudy spring day. In her memory, he wears the same weak smile she sees before her, with the same upward curl in his eyebrows. She blinks away the sweet memory and recalls the Foreman Clan's vicious attacks. "Mirna, Dianis, and Bethany... just a few of my sisters you killed."

His smile gradually transforms into a stiff frown. "Our losses equaled yours. After what your coven has been through, I would expect you to understand the heartache of losing one's entire people."

With a sigh, Patricia releases her hold on Arsen. The seconds that pass between them fill her mind with all the sisters she lost during the dragons' rebellion. The dragons nearly destroyed her coven, just as her coven nearly annihilated the Foreman Clan. Pity rises in Patricia's stomach, and she fights it off with memories of the clan's initial attack. Her sisters' screams echoing in her mind.

From Arsen's solemn stare, Patricia can only guess similar thoughts fill his mind. Centuries have passed, wars have begun and ended, dynasties have fallen, countries have formed and broken, and still the scars of betrayal linger on both sides like eternal embers unwilling to burn out. A few more seconds pass and their gazes soften. As the echoes of battle fade away,

Patricia lifts her eyes and glowers at Arsen.

"Tell me how to stop the transfer."

Arsen hears a hopeful melody in Patricia's request, a potential peace offering. He clears his throat of its sudden dryness. "There are not many possible outcomes. Either Logan kills Caderyn and becomes the clan's new leader, gaining all Caderyn's power over the clansmen, or Caderyn will kill Logan to keep his position. If the transfer completes successfully, Logan will have all of Caderyn's memories and powers."

"What if neither of them acts?"

"Theoretically, they can both exist and share their magic between them. I say 'theoretically' because it has never been done before."

"But they *can* exist at the same time, together?"

"Again, theoretically. What is definite is that they will both be weaker than the clansmen they lead since their magic is shared between them. Neither one will have full power, and what powers they would actually possess remains uncertain. And, Logan may not inherit the knowledge to execute them. There are potential consequences."

Patricia blinks away the memory of Katarina's broken body—a true consequence of Agatha's incomplete transfer of magic.

"But again, it has never been done. Our clansmen don't usually wait a long period before completing the transfer. It is when the sorcerer is at his weakest, so they usually keep the transfer period short. When Caderyn was chosen, he and his father completed the transfer within a few days, and with only a handful of clansmen as witnesses. They kept the transfer secret; they didn't want to risk losing leadership of the clan."

"How could they lose leadership?"

"Our leader is the strongest of our brothers; he possesses

powers no other brother holds. It's part of our clan's magic. However, during the transfer process, magic is moving from the sorcerer to his successor. So, during the transfer, our leader loses power, becoming a weak target. The successor has yet to receive all the leader's magic and knowledge, so he too is weak. If anyone kills both the leader and his successor before the transfer is complete, then he'll inherit the clan's leadership."

"What if I kill Caderyn?" Patricia raises one eyebrow.

Arsen presses his lips into a tight line. "If you kill Caderyn, Logan will maintain whatever he's already inherited, but he'll still be vulnerable. His abilities would be unpredictable. And when Kean learns of the transfer, he'll kill Caderyn and come after Logan."

"Why would Kean kill Caderyn?"

"It's a rather long story. Shall we sit?"

Arsen stretches his hand out toward a long metal bench between two potted ferns at one side of the hospital lobby. Patricia sits down at one corner, leans back, and crosses one leg over the other, and Arsen sits at the other end. He sighs, contemplating the changes that would occur if Kean or Caderyn were to fulfill either of their goals—dragons, battles, war, death. But his thoughts are interrupted by a sudden spray of sunlight reflecting through Patricia's stunning eyes, the mocha glow mesmerizing him.

Why did I give you up? For my family. For my brothers. For the clan. And what has it given me? I was lucky to have your love back then. Could I be so lucky now?

"Arsen?" The corner of her lips rises for a millisecond.

It's time for a change. It's time for new alliances.

He blinks twice and sighs. "What I'm about to tell you is all true."

Patricia huffs and crosses her arms tighter.

"In all our years together, you know I have never lied to you. I hide nothing from you. We are beyond keeping secrets."

Patricia holds his gaze for a few silent seconds. "Go on."

"Kean wants the clan's leadership. The only way Kean can get it is during the transfer of magic. For the last few centuries, Kean has set Caderyn up with women in the hopes of producing an heir that will trigger the transfer of power. Although Caderyn has had many sons, he has never recognized any of them as his kin. Not really. But now, it seems he has acknowledged Logan as his kin, and, consequently, through no fault of his own, our clan's magic has chosen Logan as Caderyn's heir. But, I don't think Kean has learned of it yet."

"How do you know?"

"Because Caderyn is still alive. If Kean knew, he would have killed Caderyn immediately, and I would have felt his death."

"Where is Kean now?"

"He is with Caderyn. They were scheduled to meet with Ryland in Manchester."

"Ryland still lives?"

Arsen nods. "For over a century now, he's found solace in an underground chamber of an old library in Manchester."

Patricia rolls her eyes to the side. "Evil hiding amongst the masses."

A slight grin quirks the side of Arsen's mouth. "Everyone hides their real selves amongst the masses. Even you, Patricia."

Her nostrils flare when she inhales. "Why are they meeting?"

Arsen rests his hands on his knees, his face serious again. "When the elders learned of Finna's ability to turn back time and change history—"

"I'm sorry." Patricia furrows her eyebrows and tilts her head. "Ability to do what?"

"To change history, by returning to a previous time in her own life and altering events."

She raises her eyebrows. "Finna?" She narrows her eyes at Arsen.

"Yes. Finna." Arsen sits back and returns the perplexed look. "You didn't know Finna possessed this power?"

With a flush of frustration burning hot under her skin, Patricia stands and steps away from the bench. "There is nothing I have come to loathe more in my entire life than secrets."

"The elders sensed something about Finna from the very beginning—something strong and immutable, something about her powers that could not be counterbalanced. Once Caderyn and Finna were married and had Agatha, the council warned Caderyn of their suspicions. They sensed that Finna was using her magic to betray the clan, but nothing concrete. In any case, there was no persuading Caderyn of Finna's false intentions."

Patricia whips around and glares at Arsen. "Finna was not false. She loved Caderyn. She left him because she knew Caderyn doubted her; she feared her daughter's safety. Your council members and your elders have persuaded your leaders to conquer lands, burn villages, and commit unmentionable atrocities for the sake of power and dynasty. How Finna ever trusted Caderyn in the first place is beyond me."

With the careful motions of a lion tamer, Arsen stands and gestures Patricia back onto the bench. "Please, for Logan's sake, allow me to continue."

Seconds pass as Patricia inspects every inch of Arsen's frame, down to the tips of his shoes. After a deep inhalation, Patricia meets his pleading eyes and nods. She takes a seat.

"I'll tell you what I know is true, based on Caderyn's

account and the elders' research. But, first, you have to consider that the council members acted on behalf of the clan, just as Finna acted on behalf of her coven."

Patricia nods. "Go on."

"Like many clans then, we craved power and land and all that's afforded by growing an empire. It was neither good nor bad. It just was. Those were the times."

Arsen pauses for a moment, and Patricia strengthens her glare. He huffs and shakes his head as he realizes how outrageous this will sound to Patricia, at first. He searches the lobby floor for the right words.

"Imagine, in another lifetime, our clan attacked your coven and killed everyone on your island, except for one. Finna was the sole survivor of your people. She was our captive, and we were about to execute her."

Patricia crosses her arms and legs. "Okay."

"Moments before her execution, Finna used the time-reversal spell and returned to a time long before the attacks. She remembered everything that occurred, that *would* occur, if she didn't do something to change the course of history."

Arsen sees Patricia furrow her eyebrows. He continues cautiously. "Finna knew she had to do something. So, she searched for Caderyn and enticed him into falling in love with her. She married him in hopes of preventing the attack and your coven's demise."

She huffs. "A fascinating story."

"A true story."

"Is there more?"

Arsen lowers his gaze as he gathers his thoughts. "I believe Finna's intentions at the time were noble. I spent a lot of time with them, as you know, and I believe Finna truly loved Caderyn. But, I also believe she knew the council was suspicious of her long before Caderyn made her aware of it. Their marriage was scandalous; it was the first time a clan leader had married a powerful sorceress—the leader of a coven no less. The union raised many eyebrows, and most of the elders and council members disapproved."

"It was argued about in our coven as well. No coven leader had ever married a clan leader. Mixing such enchanted bloodlines was unprecedented. But we trusted Finna's judgment."

"Yes, well you had no reason to doubt her then."

She purses her lips and narrows her eyes at Arsen.

"When Caderyn and Finna had Agatha, the clan expected more children to follow. Yet, their attempts to have more children failed. Finna had an heiress, and Caderyn had no male heir. The future of the clan was at stake, and the council became impatient. Internal rivals were voicing their opinions about the union, claiming that Caderyn was weakening under Finna's enchantments and that Finna desired control over the clan. The lack of a male heir to balance the union was a thorn in the council's side. They used it as proof of their claim. They even accused Finna of avoiding pregnancy."

Patricia huffs and shakes her head.

"The council didn't like the instability, so they continued challenging Caderyn to prove Finna's commitment and loyalty to the clan. And he trusted her. He defended her against every allegation, every wild claim his political enemies made, until..."

"Until she ran away with Agatha and the dragon eggs." Patricia rolls her eyes to the side.

"Caderyn and every other member of the clan, including myself, were convinced that the elders and council members had been correct all along. I witnessed Caderyn's pain and anger, and I'll admit that I fanned the flames of revenge." He glances down at his hands. "He wasn't the only one who felt betrayed."

When he looks up, he meets Patricia's pensive eyes.

"I've come to realize that stealing the dragon eggs was a backup plan; it was never her truest intention. Finna wanted peace. She sacrificed her previous life to marry Caderyn and create peace between our two peoples. Although her plans for peace failed, her initial plan, to prevent the destruction of her coven, was successful."

"Until the dragons rebelled."

Arsen nods and lowers his eyes once more.

"We didn't know about the dragon rebellion until almost a century after it occurred. When Kean learned there were only three of you left, he returned to search for Agatha. But, you were all gone by then."

"Why was Kean looking for Agatha?"

"Agatha is Finna's successor; therefore, she can execute the time-reversal magic. Kean wanted to go back in time to change the outcome of the war, but first, he needed Agatha's beating heart."

Patricia gasps. "The Forbidden Consumption."

"Correct. But now that Agatha is dead, Jasmyn owns that power."

Patricia uncrosses her legs and stands, glaring down at Arsen. "You're here for Jasmyn."

After a huff, Arsen leans back on the bench and shakes his head. "If I were after Jasmyn, why would I tell you all of this?" He leans forward and rests his elbows on his knees. He peeks up at Patricia. "I'm not after Jasmyn or Logan. I'm here for no one… but you."

The metallic squeal of a door hinge catches Arsen's attention. His gaze shoots to the right where Gustavo is entering the hospital lobby from the staircase. Two men in military uniforms holding automatic weapons join Gustavo as they walk toward Arsen and Patricia. Two more soldiers appear at the entrance with weapons in hand.

From across the lobby, Gustavo shouts, "These men are here to escort you off the base."

Arsen rises as Gustavo approaches, holding his stare as he studies Gustavo's intense blue aura. When Gustavo arrives at Patricia's side, Arsen notices Gustavo's aura blending with Patricia's, as his used to do. Arsen adjusts his suit's lapel and tugs on each of the jacket's sleeves. He turns his entire body to face Patricia. "I must be on my way. Caderyn is waiting."

He steps between Gustavo and Patricia, forcing Gustavo to take a step backward.

"Wait." Patricia grabs Arsen's arm.

Arsen pivots back, stares down at her hand for a second before glancing over his shoulder at Gustavo. He glances back at Patricia, and she releases her grasp.

"You said Caderyn and Kean were meeting with the elder. Why?"

Arsen's chest swells as her eyes beg him for an answer. *There is no resisting those eyes.*

"Ryland is researching how to execute your entrapment magic to release Jasmyn's dragon and place him under Caderyn's control. He is also researching ways to execute the time-reversal spell using Jasmyn's blood—without having to perform the Forbidden Consumption. Caderyn wants nothing to do with such dark magic. And although Kean has no qualms about consuming Jasmyn's heart, Caderyn has prohibited him from doing so."

"Consume Jasmyn's heart?" Gustavo glares Patricia. "What the hell is he talking about?"

Patricia shivers. "Jasmyn is the key. She holds the blood

to all of this magic. Whoever consumes the beating heart of a sorcerer will inherit their powers."

"Caderyn doesn't want to perform the Forbidden Consumption, which is why he asked the elder to do more research. But… as soon as Kean realizes the transfer has started, he'll kill Caderyn and come after Logan for the clan's leadership. Then he'll go after Jasmyn to consume her heart. Kean is the one you should be worried about."

He glances at the two soldiers behind Gustavo and then back at Patricia. "Now, if you'll excuse me, I must get back to Caderyn."

"What will you tell him about our meeting?"

A warm smile crosses Arsen's face as he loses himself in her cinnamon eyes. "I'll tell him everything, and I'll take what's coming to me." Leaning in close, he whispers, "I, too, loathe secrets."

A moment passes in silence as Arsen and Patricia stare at each other. He lifts her right hand and plants a kiss on the back of her wrist before she can protest. "Until next we meet."

After a long stare at Patricia, Arsen turns to Gustavo and huffs at his bold, blue aura illuminated with solid streaks of light he seldom sees in men these days. After another glance back at Patricia, he faces Gustavo once more. "You are a knight amongst men, Gustavo. A rare specimen indeed. I see why she cares for you." He looks at the two soldiers next to Gustavo. "Since you two are assigned to follow me, would you be so kind as to give me a ride to the airport? I'll be on the first flight out of town."

Gustavo nods and the two soldiers walk out of the hospital lobby with Arsen walking between them. Once they get in the Hummer and drive away, Patricia sits down on the bench and exhales.

9

UNEASINESS

"Those soldiers won't try anything, will they? He'll kill them if they do."

Gustavo sits down next to Patricia. "They're just going to make sure he leaves."

"We have to get Jasmyn and Logan together. There's a lot to go over."

"Are you sure it's okay to let him go?"

"We have to. If anyone can persuade Caderyn in our favor, it's him." Patricia shrugs her shoulders. "He's already told us more than he should have. Caderyn will surely be vexed. Arsen is under Caderyn's control, and he will disclose everything about our encounter even if he doesn't want to. He won't be able to hide the fact that he shared his clan's secrets with me."

A bemused look crosses Gustavo's face. "Why would he help us?"

"My guess is… after centuries of being under the physical and mental control of another sorcerer, Arsen has grown tired of it. You begin to question the meaning of existence, of relationships, the very definition of life and purpose. Maybe, seeing me after all this time brought back memories and emotions that he's long missed. Love and hate make people do crazy things."

Patricia stares at the floor and concentrates on the tidal wave of information Arsen has given her.

Finna did love Caderyn. I know it. But what was Finna

supposed to do? Her daughter meant the world to her. She had to keep her safe. If only his council would have left them alone.

She shakes her head.

What would Finna have done if Caderyn took Agatha away from her? I would undoubtedly have urged her to go to war, fanned the flames of revenge. I would have attacked the clan and killed every single one of them.

After a sigh, Patricia opens her eyes and leans her head back on the wall behind the bench. "No matter how much time passes, the past continues to startle me."

"Did you love him?" Gustavo asks.

Patricia lifts her head and turns to face him. A perplexed look crosses her face. "What?"

Gustavo shrugs his shoulders and rolls his eyes. "He obviously cares about you."

She glances down at the floor and then looks up at Gustavo. "Love has a different meaning when you're young and naive."

"I want to make sure *you* won't do anything… crazy."

With her cheeks blooming with a hint of a smile, Patricia stands up. "You don't have to worry about me. I'm under no one's control, and I have people in my life. When you think about it, the emptiness of his existence—no love to speak of, familial or otherwise, no relations, no true happiness, and living under the control of another—you might find yourself feeling pity for someone like Arsen."

Gustavo shrugs his shoulders. "Maybe."

~ ~ ~

As Jasmyn gazes at the lush trees on the mountain range surrounding the quiet lake, she can't help but wonder if she could move them. She recites a mountain-moving spell, but it fails to execute. After a sigh, she bends down to pick up three tiny rocks and whips her arm sideways, sending the rocks into flight across the surface of the lake. A soft plop reverberates after each bounce. She whispers another spell to call the stone back to her hand but fails again.

I guess magic doesn't work in my dreams.

Two more rocks follow the path of circular ripples, and after three hops they, too, sink to the bottom. As the waves fade, Jasmyn turns around to face Katarina sitting on a rock behind her.

Why is that? Why won't any of my spells work here?

Katarina's stretches her right arm down to draw a circular figure in the sand with a long twig. Swirls and round shapes take form as she jabs the wiry branch into the ground and drags it along.

Jasmyn bends down to pick up more rocks.

So many rules. So trivial. Why not allow me to execute spells in my dreams? I mean, I know I'm dreaming, and I know all this is not real; it's all concocted in my mind. So why can't I move that mountain? Why shouldn't I be allowed to move the lake's water or these little rocks?

With her hand outstretched to show Katarina the pebbles, Jasmyn steps toward her sister.

These insignificant, tiny, meaningless specks of stone; why can't I just move them?

With the grace of a ballerina, Katarina slides down the rock and walks to the lake's sandy shoreline. Her white frock, trimmed with yellow daisies at the hem, whips in the wind as she steps into the water. She continues until she is neck-deep, then turns around to swim backward into the lake's dark center. After a few long strokes, Katarina lifts her eyes to meet Jasmyn's worried gaze. Then, in a heartbeat, Katarina goes under.

Jasmyn gasps and sits up in her bed, beads of sweat trickling down her forehead. After glancing at Brian who's sleeping on top of the bedspread next to her, she crawls out from under her quilt and perches at the edge of her side of the bed. She grips the edge of the mattress tightly and tenses her arm muscles.

Why won't she speak to me?

Brian stirs and mumbles, "Nightmare?"

"Not really. Just a dream."

"Was Kat in it?"

"Yeah."

He rubs his eyes. "Did she say anything to you?"

Pressing her lips together and staring down at her feet, Jasmyn replays her dream in her mind, picturing every minute detail down to the footprints Katarina left in the sand at the shore of the lake. Her body trembles when she recalls how the footprints disappeared, erased by a gentle gust of wind.

"Not a word."

Brian sits up and stretches his arms toward the ceiling, and then removes his sweater and folds it neatly by the window pane. After rolling his shoulders and twisting his back, he sinks back down onto the bed and closes his eyes. The sun peeks in through the blinds and shines next to his face, as if summoning him to wake up, but he turns his face away from the sun's rays.

With his eyes closed, he mumbles into the pillow, "Just another few minutes, and then we'll check in with Patricia and get some food."

She lays down next to Brian and places her head on his shoulder. In response, Brian stretches out his left arm to accommodate Jasmyn's snuggle and wraps his arm around her shoulder. The warm vibrations emanating from Brian's aura relax her tense muscles.

"She looked at me," Jasmyn whispers. She rubs her head on his chest, wiping a single tear on his T-shirt. "She looked at me, and then she disappeared under the water. I'm not sure if she dove down or if she was pulled under. Either way, the thought makes me sick."

Brian sighs. "You're still punishing yourself."

"Maybe."

"It was just a dream." He yawns.

"My dreams are never 'just dreams.'"

~ ~ ~

The repetitive *buzz* coming from the bedside table jars Brian from a deep sleep. He finds himself lying on his side and holding Jasmyn with both arms. Her head is burrowed deep into his chest, and her left leg wraps around his right hip. His cell phone vibrates again, and as much as he wants to stay in his current position, he carefully rolls out of Jasmyn's embrace to answer the call.

"Hello?"

"Are you sleeping?" Patricia asks.

"Yeah. We're both asleep," he whispers. Patricia doesn't respond right away, and he wonders if his words have given her a wrong impression. "I mean—"

"Wake Jasmyn up. There's a lot to do. We're heading over now."

He turns back to Jasmyn and sighs at the thought of having to wake her. The silkiness of her wavy hair brushes against his fingers as he pulls several strands back away from her face. His mind records the curves of her cheeks, the edges of her eyebrows, the curl in her eyelashes, the freckles on her nose, and other minute features.

He concentrates on her pink lips and notices a slight downward curve at the edges, and a wrinkle in between her eyebrows indicative of concern. Even in her sleep, her pain is evident. Brian's heart aches, wishing he could do something to help her stop hurting.

He nudges her shoulder. "Wake up. Everyone's coming over," he whispers.

Jasmyn rolls onto her back.

"What were you dreaming about?"

"Same dream. Kat going under the water."

With a sigh, Brian throws himself back onto the bed and stares up at the ceiling. "You were frowning in your sleep. You looked like you were about to cry."

Jasmyn nods. "It's a horrible dream."

Brian turns onto his side and faces Jasmyn. He moves closer to her and whispers, "Do you want me to wake you the next time I see that you're having a nightmare?"

She turns on her side to face him, also inching closer. "If you did, I'd never sleep."

They lay there for another minute with their eyes closed, breathing deeply.

Jasmyn soaks in the warmth of his aura. She sighs as she recalls Brian's laughter as he played guinea pig for her elemental spells. Every time he fell victim to one of her blunders, he got up, dusted himself off, chuckled, and told Jasmyn to try again. And again, she did.

Guilt laces the drops of happiness she feels, and she presses her lips into a straight line and contemplates moving away. But Brian's pull intensifies, drowning out her hesitation. She shifts closer—her face only inches away from his. Brian's body heat, his aura's vibrations, and the sound of his breathing lulls Jasmyn. She fights the narcoleptic effect, opens her eyes, and concentrates her stare on his lips.

After a few seconds of fighting his desire to kiss her, a frustration he has come to know well, Brian rolls onto his back and exhales a lungful of air. He sits up at the edge of his side of the bed and sighs once more. "They're going to be here any minute."

Jasmyn pulls herself up to a sitting position. "Right." She tugs on her boots, keeping her head low to hide the heat rising on her face. She stands up and walks out of the room before Brian can say anything else.

10

REMINISCING

When Jasmyn answers the door, her mouth drops open. "Logan?"

"Hey, Jaz."

She stares, speechless for a few seconds, before asking, "What are you doing here?"

"Patricia wanted Nana's stuff. So…" Logan shrugs his shoulders.

Jasmyn braces herself for the daggers, the knives, the piercing sensation that ripped through her skin the last time she saw him. But, to Jasmyn's surprise, a blanketing warmth exudes from her brother's aura. His eyebrows arch high above an apologetic smile as he struggles with the heavy box in his arms.

"Where can I put this?" He grunts as he adjusts the box to a new position. A skinny young man wearing a tan uniform stands behind him, also struggling with a taped box. Logan drops his box on the kitchen counter and gestures for the young man to follow suit.

Brian strides up behind Logan and throws an arm around his shoulders. Jasmyn looks away, uncomfortably jealous at Brian's effortless warmth toward her brother. She slides onto a stool at the island counter.

"Can you help Henry with the other boxes?" Logan asks.

Brian nods, glances at Jasmyn, and then leaves with Henry to get the other boxes from the truck. When the front door closes, Logan clears his throat. "I hear you're quite the sorceress these days. Moving mountains and desert floors." He drops onto a stool across the counter from her.

A self-conscious chill crosses Jasmyn's arms, and she rubs her biceps. "I can do a few things, but I'm still figuring it out." Shrugging her shoulders. "How are Mom and Dad?"

"They're as good as can be expected, I guess."

Jasmyn nods, still unable to make full eye contact, and folds her hands on her lap.

"I told Dad that I'd, somehow, convince you to come home."

She shakes her head. "I can't."

"Why not? It's still your home." He leans in and dips his head under her eyes to get her attention, but she looks away again.

"I can't go back and live there as if nothing has changed. I can't see Kat's room, her toys, her bed…" The tightness in her throat kills her voice as she pictures Katarina spinning around in front of her princess-themed mirror, with a pink blanket tied around her neck, pretending to be a superhero princess fighting crime and ruling the land. She presses her eyes shut. "I just can't."

At that instant, Logan straightens his back as he remembers why he started on his trip in the first place. "Maybe you won't have to." He pulls Jasmyn's journal from the corner of the box on the counter. As Jasmyn's eyes narrow at the sight of the journal, he raises a hand in surrender. "Now, don't get mad, but I was getting worried about you, so I poked around in your room."

"I can't believe you—"

"I didn't plan to read your journal." He glances down at the journal and then back at his sister. "I was looking at your drawings and painting, looking for a way to… get through to you. You're not exactly the most approachable person in the world."

Jasmyn's mouth opens, but she's unable to speak.

Logan hands her the journal. "And I only read the last entry, which you wrote the day Nana died. Do you remember what you wrote?"

Blinking rapidly, Jasmyn recalls her anger and loneliness as she wrote about Katarina taking her grandmother's dragon medallion. She remembers feeling jealous when Katarina and Logan rummaged through her grandmother's collection without her. Her chest fills with air so thick it's hard to breathe or swallow.

With as casual a motion as she can manage, Jasmyn turns around with her journal in her hand and steps toward the couch. When she sits down, she opens her journal to the page holding the satin bookmark.

Her eyes well up as she focuses in on the entry, on the putrid words describing those terrible, regretted emotions. On the page is evidence that she kept a precious story from Katarina, a story Katarina was so eager to learn, a story Katarina will never hear. Self-hatred washes over Jasmyn as tears roll down her cheeks, her envy and hatred screaming out from the page. And after reading those few short sentences, Jasmyn closes her eyes and relives the two pivotal moments of that day—when she destroyed the box containing the dragon souls, and when Katarina died in her arms.

All because of a stupid dragon medallion. All because I wanted to keep this story from you. I should have died, Kat, not you. I should have died.

Jasmyn breaks into a deep sob, and her brother rushes over to the couch and wraps his right arm around her shoulders.

"I was so mean to her," Jasmyn cries. "I was so horrible

to her, and all she wanted to know was the freaking story tied to the goddamned dragon medallion, and I wouldn't tell her. I was so, so… evil. I wouldn't tell her the story. All I had to do was share the story with her, make her happy, and I didn't. And now… it's all my fault."

"No, it isn't, Jaz." Logan sits back. "We're all to blame."

Jasmyn stops sobbing and looks up at her brother, mouth agape.

"I should have said something to Mom and Dad about how they treated you. I should have stood up for you more. I should have stepped in sooner, tried to fix things between you and Kat, or at least included you when…" Logan's eyes well up.

She wipes her face. "Logan—"

"I just stood by and let things happen," he says in a hoarse voice as he stands up and heads to the kitchen. After pacing for a few seconds, he turns on the sink to wash his hands and face. He leans back against the counter with his arms folded across his chest, his lips pressed into a tight line, breathing heavily through his nostrils.

After a few minutes, Logan takes a deep breath and heads back to the couch.

"In the last journal entry, you wrote a story about Nana's dragon medallion, about a time-reversal spell. Was it a true story?"

Jasmyn shrugs her shoulders. "I don't know if it was a *true* story or just something Nana made up. All of her stories are in the *Book of Whispers*, except that one." She scans the room and the ceiling. "I don't have Nana's memories, I inherited Patricia's, and I don't recall anything about a time-reversal spell in Patricia's memories."

The apartment door opens, and Brian walks in holding a box. Porcelain and crystal objects clatter inside the box when he sets it down on the kitchen table. Henry walks in carrying Regina. He sets her down on a stool at the kitchen counter.

"Thank you, Henry." Regina bats her eyelashes. "I hope we'll be seeing you again."

Henry places his hand flat on his chest and bows. "I'm at your service, Miss Meyer." He smiles to one side. "Your wheelchair is just outside the door. If you need anything else, you have my number."

"I'll be calling you soon enough."

As Patricia walks in, she catches the flutter of Regina's eyelashes and rolls her eyes. Gustavo walks in behind Patricia and clears his throat, holding the apartment door open.

Henry's grin reverts to military professionalism. "I'll be in the truck."

As the door clicks shut, Patricia shakes her head at Regina. "You are unbelievable."

"Why, thank you." Regina adjusts herself at the counter to face the living room. "You know, we don't do enough to thank our servicemen. Don't you agree, Patricia?"

Gustavo chuckles, and Patricia ignores them both. When she sees Logan sitting on the couch next to Jasmyn, she moves to the living room and sits on the coffee table across from them. "A happy reunion, I see."

Both Logan and Jasmyn offer Patricia a weak smile.

Patricia sighs. "And I haven't even explained that both of you are being hunted."

Their eyebrows furrow in confusion.

"Jasmyn too? Why?"

"Because, apparently, she has the ability to reverse time, and that is something Kean wants desperately."

"Kean?" Jasmyn narrows her eyes as the memories she inherited from Patricia unravel the mystery. She sees a man named Kean, standing with his hands clasped, behind Caderyn and other men at a union ceremony. "He was part of the Foreman Clan, right?"

Patricia and Logan share a knowing glance. "He *is* part of the clan. And Caderyn, who we thought was dead, is still alive."

Jasmyn sits up, her eyes searching the floor wildly. Like a video in fast-forward, visions of Caderyn and Kean and other men replay themselves in her thoughts. There are ceremonies, gatherings, romantic moments with a man named Arsen, arguments among the older, more established women of her coven about a union, treachery, betrayal, and then a war. She clenches her shirt as she sees the Foreman Clan attacking and killing her sisters. Patricia's pain roots itself inside Jasmyn, and mixed emotions arise when she sees the dragons coming to the coven's defense.

"What about the other members of the clan?" Jasmyn finally asks once Patricia's memories fade into more modern times. "Are they still alive?"

Patricia shares a knowing glance with Logan. "There's a few left, and they're coming for both of you."

11

TAKING SIDES

At the airport, Arsen finally calls Caderyn, but Kean answers.

"Kean?" Arsen pulls his mobile phone away from his face to verify that he dialed the correct number. He did. "Where's Caderyn?"

"He's turned in for the night."

"Why do you have his phone?"

"Because we're awaiting your update. What news do you have?"

"There were no dragon eggs in Agatha's possessions." Arsen sits back in his chair in the airport lounge.

"And what about the entrapment case holding the dragon?"

"I don't have it."

"You mean to tell me that you, Arsen, son of the great Jorgen, could not take a small box from a child?"

"At eighteen years of age, people of our kind are hardly children. Besides, I didn't see the girl. She wasn't at Agatha's home."

"Was anyone there?"

"Logan, Agatha's grandson."

"Logan?" A pause. "Did you sense anything strange about him?"

"Hold on; my drink has arrived."

Arsen pulls the phone away from his face and reaches

for his gin on the table. With the gin warming the insides of his throat and stomach, Arsen closes his eyes and sighs.

If I tell Kean the truth, he will immediately kill Caderyn and go after Logan. Kean becomes the clan's new leader, with me in his favor, and Patricia will probably die defending Logan.

He takes another sip of his gin.

If I lie to Kean, it will buy Caderyn time. He can go after Logan to regain his full power. And, again, Patricia might die defending Logan. Or...

One more sip.

Caderyn might decide to complete the transfer and hand over his powers to his great-grandson. And since Logan is Finna's kin, maybe...

His chest swells at the possibility.

Maybe we can finally have peace with the coven.

After finishing his drink, he places the empty glass down at the table and orders another. "I apologize for the wait. What were we discussing? Oh yes. Agatha's grandson, Logan. I didn't notice anything strange about him. Why?"

"Pity. I thought I saw Caderyn wavering earlier."

"You shouldn't plot against him, Kean."

"He's been our dormant leader for centuries, with nothing to boast from it. Instead of growing our numbers as only our leader can, Caderyn has been idling in contemplation, hiding behind normalcy, dealing with these mortals, these insignificant people, and for what?"

"He calls it peace."

"Peace is weakness."

"Kean, I've asked you time and time again. Don't talk ill of Caderyn. He is my brother, as are you. Don't make me choose sides."

"How can you even consider defending him?"

Arsen rises to his feet. "Because *you* are attacking *him*. I would defend you in the same way if it were the other way around. You are both my brothers."

Arsen hears Kean huff over the call.

"Caderyn is capable of ending you, and you continue with your plotting. Even after I warned him about your plans decades ago, he still let you live."

"Evidence of his weakness."

"I begged him to!" Arsen growls into the phone, his teeth clenching. "You're still alive because I begged Caderyn to forgive you, you ungrateful wretch. And still you plot!"

After a few seconds, Arsen regains his composure and shakes the tension from his shoulders. He sits back down and sips from his freshly-poured glass of gin.

Kean clears his throat. "Arsen, brother, allow me to try to explain my intentions. I don't want to be at odds with you. I just need you to understand."

The ice cubes in the glass *clink* when Arsen places it down on the table. He waves his hand at the bartender and points at his glass, ordering another drink. "Fine. Go on."

"Throughout centuries, our clan has ruled with power. We've conquered lands and overthrown our enemies, for the greatness of our people. We've apologized to no one."

Arsen rolls his eyes and shakes his head.

"One lost war, one defeat, and Caderyn, our great leader, crumbles. It's shameful. It's a dishonor to our people, to our ancestors. We're not meant to exist this way. We're not meant to make peace with ants. We're meant to rule them. We're meant to crush them!"

Arsen rises to his feet and shakes his head, ready to reprimand Kean again for ranting against Caderyn, but he holds back.

Let him vent. Let him lose control. Don't lose it. Don't give anything more away.

"What would our ancestors say about Caderyn's behavior these past two centuries? About his legacy? How could you justify it to our ancestors? Would you defend Caderyn? Would you make excuses for him? Would our ancestors be proud?"

Although Arsen's hands are balled into tight fists, he replies in a calm tone. "You're right." He tilts his head from shoulder to shoulder to stretch his neck muscles. "Our ancestors would be ashamed of Caderyn's behavior."

"I can't just sit back and watch him destroy our legacy and the legacy of our ancestors." Kean sighs and continues in a less agitated tone. "Do you understand me now? I'm not plotting against Caderyn, not as I did long ago, but, if Caderyn's heir is chosen, then we must take advantage of the opportunity. We owe it to our ancestors!"

The bartender places a drink down in front of Arsen, and Arsen consumes it in one gulp. The light bouncing off the side of the glass grabs Arsen's attention, reflecting orange-gold rays of the setting sun shining in through the lounge's windows. He walks over to the window and is transfixed by an airplane about to lift off. He follows it until it is high into the sky, defying gravity's pull.

"I understand you, brother." Arsen rolls his eyes. "But, until that day comes, we must stay united. Agreed?"

"Yes, of course. Agreed." Kean releases an exasperated sigh. "We must stay united. There are still five of us left. The dragons didn't completely eliminate us; they..."

Arsen furrows his eyebrows when he hears Kean gasp.

Kean slowly whispers, "The dragons didn't eliminate us."

"No, they didn't. What of it?"

A burst of energy comes through in Kean's rushed tone. "I thought I would be the phoenix rising from Caderyn's ashes, but I was wrong. It took me this long, all these centuries to find the solution to our problem. I wasn't meant to be the phoenix. Caderyn will not burn. Arsen, brother, this is the start of a new era. It's time for a new beginning to this story."

"A new beginning?"

"Find the entrapment case at once." Kean commands. "I... we need that dragon. Logan or Jasmyn must have the entrapment case. They wouldn't leave it unprotected."

"This is no easy task. Patricia is with them."

"Oh?" Kean snorts. "Oh... I see."

Arsen grimaces.

"Now I see what's happened."

"Nothing has happened, Kean. Logan didn't have the case. I followed him to Nevada, and that's where I ran into Patricia, and—"

"And Patricia distracted you."

Pacing the floor of the lounge and staring at the dash pattern on the blue commercial rug, Arsen fails to come up with a rebuttal.

"Not to worry," Kean says. "Come back to Manchester. I'll send Granger or Breccan to fetch the box. They won't have a problem with Patricia or that child witch."

"No, don't bother. I'll fetch the box."

Kean chuckles. "Are you sure you're up for it?"

"Yes. Consider it done."

"Good. I'm meeting with Ryland now. Call me when the box is in your possession, and you've left the states."

After Kean ends the call, Arsen sits back and contemplates the state of affairs. Patricia's coy smile flickers into his mind, and cinnamon sparkles shine in her eyes. Once again, he is mesmerized. As he finishes his gin, Arsen presses his eyes shut and shakes his head to remove Patricia from his thoughts and reviews his conversation with Kean once more.

Kean gasped for a moment. Why?

He crunches the last bits of ice in the back of his mouth.

What changed? What was that before his gasp? 'The dragons didn't completely eradicate us.'

He raises his arm and shakes his empty glass to order one last drink.

And what's this phoenix that rises from Caderyn's ashes?

A new server walks over to his table. "I'm sorry to bother you sir, but the man who served you left without entering your drinks on the computer. I'll have to restart your order." The server waits for Arsen's response, but Arsen stares into space, repeating Kean's words over and over in his mind.

A new beginning. A restart. A new era.

Arsen's jaw drops once he realizes Kean's plan.

No. He wouldn't. He shakes his head. *Of course, he would!*

He waves the server off with one hand while the other dials rapidly into his phone. The Manchester hotel receptionist readily agrees to connect him to Caderyn's room.

~ ~ ~

Two short rings from the hotel telephone on the side table wake Caderyn from his sleep. With a lumbering stretch, he plucks the phone off the bedside table and mumbles a greeting.

"I hoped you were awake."

"I wasn't." Caderyn rubs his eyes.

"Are you alone?"

"Yes."

"Is Kean in the room with you?"

"No."

"I called your phone to speak to you, but Kean answered it. There's much to discuss. Are you fully awake, or should I give you a few minutes?"

"I'm fine." Caderyn grunts as he rises to a seated position on the bed. "Go on."

"I've met Logan. I know what's happening. I know he's been chosen. I've seen his visions, your memories."

Caderyn's mouth goes dry. He closes his eyes as the sinking sensation passes. "Does Kean know?"

"He suspected it, but when he asked me if I noticed anything odd in Logan, I told him I didn't. His intentions are not in your favor. If he finds out…"

"I keep Kean close for a reason. Now, tell me everything, exactly as it's occurred since you went to Agatha's home."

As Arsen outlines the details of the day, images trickle into Caderyn's mind. He sees Logan pulling his hair at the side of the road as he struggles with the transfer, and Arsen trying to explain everything and gaining his trust. The iridescent glow in Patricia's eyes when Arsen first saw her, and the hypnotic effect of Patricia's lips while they spoke. Patricia's frustration at learning new truths, and Arsen's ability to calm her rage—an ability that may be useful in the future.

Unlike Kean whose stories cause ripples and waves in their associated images, Arsen's images are always clear and steady, free of manipulation. Caderyn has always counted on Arsen for his honest recollections.

The thunderstorm outside the hotel window draws

Caderyn's attention as Arsen finishes his tale. Lightning flashes, followed by a thunderclap and another burst of rain slamming against the window.

Arsen clears his throat. "I hope I was not out of line by sharing our clan's dealings with Patricia. It was in the interest of gaining her trust. If I have acted incorrectly, Caderyn, please accept my sincerest apologies."

"There's no need to apologize. I'm amazed that Finna or Agatha didn't reveal more to her coven than she did. But, I'm interested in knowing your intentions with regard to Patricia. At first, she was hostile toward you, and yet, you didn't fight back."

"Even after all that has transpired between our two clans, I can't justify any hatred toward Patricia or her coven. I haven't thought about her in a long while." Arsen breathes deeply as he remembers the energy that coursed through his body when he met with Patricia. "When I saw her today, I was stunned."

"I suppose, knowing what we know now, I too would be stunned if I saw Finna before me." Caderyn reaches for the onyx ring around his finger and turns it. The smooth, black onyx stone circling his finger sparkles under the flash of another lightning strike. "My father wore this ring, and his father before him," Caderyn whispers to himself.

"Caderyn?"

The image of Finna when he last saw her still gives him shivers—Finna standing in her white frock, holding Agatha in her arms, with her golden tresses draped over her shoulders. "All things take their course. I led. I fought. I won." He swallows hard as he hears Agatha's infant laughter, the incoherent but delightful mumbles of a feisty toddler, and the squeals of a child in the throes of pure happiness. The sweet sounds fade into nothing. "And, I have lost."

"Have you met with Ryland yet?" Arsen asks, breaking

Caderyn's reverie.

"We are meeting with Ryland in the morning. He needed time to prepare his findings on the coven's sorcery."

"I just spoke to Kean. He's meeting with Ryland right now."

"Are you certain?"

"I believe he plans on using the dragons against you."

"He said this?"

"No, but why else would he meet Ryland without you? Also, you talked to Ryland about possibly executing Finna's time-reversal spell, correct?"

"Yes, if we could use it without performing the Forbidden Consumption. To return to the time before the war with the coven. To change the course of history."

"I believe Kean has other plans."

Caderyn pauses. "Has he mentioned something?"

"Kean said, and I quote, 'It's time for a new beginning to this story.' He has no qualms about consuming Jasmyn's heart, and I believe he'll use Jasmyn's time-reversal spell to go as far back as your transfer ceremony. He and I were both there as witnesses. He can change the course of our entire existence."

Caderyn narrows his eyes as he ponders the depth of Kean's betrayal. "Brotherhood and bloodlines aside, I should have dispatched Kean ages ago." He shakes his head and stares up at the stormy night sky. "I truly hoped time would smooth out the wrinkles of our past, give him some peace, but it seems peace and forgiveness are out of his reach."

"Finna chose you, Caderyn. There was nothing to forgive."

"And our clan's magic chose my father over his. Kean's father was the eldest in the family. He was supposed to be chosen as clan leader."

"That was long before your time, and, once again, neither you nor Kean had a choice in the matter. As your blood cousin, Kean should have absolved you of all your so-called crimes."

"It's easy for us to say such things. We were not cheated."

Complete silence settles over the call for a few seconds. Caderyn shakes his head at his disappointment, both in Kean's actions and in himself for not killing him while his powers allowed him to. At half-strength now, he knows he wouldn't stand a chance against Kean.

"What is your plan with Logan—now that the transfer is underway?"

Caderyn presses his lips together as he recalls his father words the night before his transfer ceremony.

"Caderyn," Arsen exhales, "if you tell me to kill Logan so you can keep the leadership, then I'll obey your order. But... I've met Logan, and..."

"And?"

"He's very much as you used to be when you were his age. It's brought back some emotions."

"I have to admit, seeing Agatha's face on the news has filled me with the same sentimentality."

"Her name is Jasmyn."

Caderyn huffs and smirks. "So, it seems."

"She is remarkably similar to your daughter, and Logan is a younger version of you. I... I feel very protective of him."

"Are we that much alike?"

"Down to the same stubbornness."

Caderyn chuckles, and Arsen joins in. It fills Caderyn with a warmth he hasn't felt in a long time.

After a few seconds of silence, Arsen sighs. "I worry for

both Logan and Jasmyn's safety. She's your great-granddaughter, Finna and Agatha's heir. There is no denying it. Logan is your great-grandson and now the heir to your powers. As much as it pains me to think of your departure, it will pain me more if both you and Logan perish. By delaying the transfer further, you are risking your life and your legacy. Kean will erase your relationship with Finna, Agatha, and the rest of your lineage. All that you remember, all that you know, will be gone."

Lightning flashes outside Caderyn's hotel window, with thunder rumbling in reply. The dark gray clouds stretch beyond the city lights. Rainfall rattles against the window as if desperate to get inside. Caderyn leans against the windowsill and focuses on the rain trickling down the pane.

The clouds produce millions of raindrops in a single storm. I had only one raindrop, Agatha, and now Jasmyn and Logan. And you, Kean, would wipe them all out in an instant.

The howling wind is replaced by the sound of delighted giggles from two-year-old Agatha and the memory of holding her high above his head as the spring breeze brushes her wavy hair back away from her face. The image of young Agatha disappears and is replaced by a powerful sorceress on a mountain summit, striking down his own army with blows of magic.

And now he sees Jasmyn's face from the news videos reciting a spell to entrap the dragon—a perfect replica of his own daughter's strength and beauty.

Generations and centuries have passed, and Finna's legacy continues in young Jasmyn. My great-granddaughter, Finna's great-granddaughter. Our great-granddaughter. Jasmyn…

He repeats her name over and over in his head.

And Logan is my great-grandson, my heir. My legacy.

The image of his father dying in his own arms flashes

before his eyes.

Will Logan feel a great loss at my death? He won't know me, but surely, he's seen some of my history, my miseries with Finna and Agatha, and my regrets. What will my life reveal to him once he receives all of my memories? Have I lived a life worthy of a legacy, as my father did before me, and his father did before him?

A bright streak of lightning catches Caderyn's attention as it crosses the dark sky. It strikes a tree and splits it in half, creating a fiery blaze. Caderyn huffs and closes his eyes.

Maybe not, but you will, Logan. You will live an honorable life.

"Thank you, Arsen, for your honesty." Caderyn eyes his own reflection in the hotel window. The dark blue aura has grown brighter and stronger throughout the conversation—the aura of his bloodline.

"What are your orders, Caderyn?" Arsen asks in a patient tone.

Caderyn clears his throat. "Go to Patricia and tell her everything. I'll be in New York City as soon as possible, and I'll call you from another line. My time in this world is coming to an end."

"And Kean?"

"Kean is dead to me."

12

MEN OF HONOR

Kean turns around the corner of a stone building and walks through a tall, thick hedge into a secret alleyway. He stops abruptly when he encounters a tall, wide-shouldered man in a charcoal robe. The robe's hood extends far over the man's forehead, hiding his face in a shadow. The hooded man bows his head slightly as Kean approaches, and then leads him into an even tighter alley, ripe with grimy puddles, fleeing vermin, and a putrid stench.

As the light of the street lamp fades behind them, a pale light glows ahead. A burst of wind rushes through the alley, picking up a discarded plastic bag and twirling it up in the air. Loose garbage scatters along the path, following the wind's guidance. The mob of storm clouds allows a faint streak of moonlight to flicker through below.

The slender passageway ends at a hickory door lined by a black metal strip. The hooded man slams his closed fist on the door firmly, waits two seconds, and then pounds the door once more. As the post-rain fog creeps into the alley, Kean lifts his suit cuff and glances at his watch. After a minute, metal latches on the door *click* and *clank* as someone on the other side unlocks them. Old hinges moan as the door opens.

The hooded man stands to the side and gestures for Kean to proceed. Another hooded man waits for him past the entrance.

After flexing and releasing his shoulder muscles, Kean walks into the chamber. The scent of burning oils infiltrates his lungs as the door behind him closes with an echoing *thud*. When Kean turns around to face his guide, he sees no one.

After a moment, his eyes adjust to the darkness. He proceeds toward a spiral staircase illuminated by small metal braziers at every fifth step down. The staircase flows into an immense underground chamber with a large circular chandelier of candles hanging from the ceiling. Arrangements of flaming torches stand at each corner of the room.

Ryland's voice booms across the vast room, inviting him in. Kean strolls down the stair, his mouth practically salivating at the possibilities Ryland presents. He reaches out his right arm and grabs Ryland's forearm in a clansman's greeting. His left hand swings over to pat Ryland's back.

After centuries of waiting, Kean is ready to fulfill his destiny.

~ ~ ~

Although Ryland is somewhat surprised by Caderyn's absence, he accepts Kean's embrace. When Kean releases him, Ryland leads the way to four mahogany leather armchairs with tall armrests that arc outward like smooth ocean waves. At the center of the seating area stands a thick piece of a tree trunk serving as a table, with clear rings circling the center and its raw, uneven edges splintering at the trunk's outer layer.

Ryland turns to face Kean. "It's been decades. You haven't changed since I last saw you. When was that? Seventy-two?"

"Seventy-five." Kean smiles. "My sideburns were much longer then."

"And so were mine." Ryland chuckles. "Shall we have a drink to warm up from the storm?"

The full dark hair on Ryland's head matches the bold black color of his eyes. He reaches down to pick up a diamond-shaped glass bottle, which he dusted off when he received Kean's late-night call. He pours the liquid into two short glasses, places two large ice cubes in each glass, and hands one to Kean.

Kean sips his drink and releases a sigh. "You've always had great taste in liquor."

"Only the finest for my esteemed guests." After placing the glass bottle down, Ryland gestures for Kean to take a seat. "I must admit, I was surprised at receiving your call. Were we not meeting tomorrow?"

Kean sets his empty glass down and sits in the chair opposite Ryland. "Yes, but I couldn't wait until morning."

Ryland unbuttons his jacket and sits. "And where is Caderyn?"

"He's resting in his hotel room. He's had a long day of travel."

"Won't he be joining us?"

"You needn't worry yourself over Caderyn."

Ryland leans back in his seat, the ice cube floating and tumbling in the liquor as he sways his glass in a circular motion. He looks down at his glass, avoiding Kean's stare, when he asks, "He is still the leader of your clan, is he not?"

"That is technically still the case. But, my plans have changed."

"I see." Ryland glances up at Kean. "And your brothers, what do they have to say about your plans?"

Kean smirks. "They'll agree soon enough. But, we must move quickly."

Ryland sips his drink and adjusts himself in his seat, wondering whose side to take, or whether to take any side at all. He leans back in his seat and meets Kean's stare. "What's your plan?"

"I will consume Jasmyn's heart, and use Finna's time-reversal spell myself."

"And how far back do you intend to go?"

"To Caderyn's transfer ceremony."

The torches flicker as silence falls over the chamber. Ryland reviews all the facts: Finna's kin is alive, Caderyn's kin is in position, and Kean's conniving proves he's unaware of the ongoing transfer of Caderyn's powers.

Ryland smirks slightly. *Oh, how one ounce of information can change your decisions. Let's see where this takes us.*

He clears his throat. "Very well. From our research, we've learned that there are two parts to Finna's time-reversal spell. First, it can only be executed from the Isle of Enid, which, as you may or may not know, is hidden under an enchantment. Caderyn requested this when we first discovered the spell's existence."

Kean narrows his eyes. "He hid the Isle of Enid?"

"Yes. A measure taken to prevent a re-occurrence of the spell, should Finna's kin ever choose to execute it. You'll need Caderyn to remove the cloak. It's a blood spell, and only he or his kin can remove it."

"And if he won't?"

"Then, perhaps there are other ways. However, I haven't researched them. I didn't know I needed to, until now."

Ryland matches Kean's glare with an unapologetic gaze. A twitch in Kean's lip gives Ryland a sense of power, but he hides his victory as he takes another sip.

"Go on."

"The second part you already know—you will need to consume the heart of Finna's kin to inherit the time-reversal spell. But, I warn you, the Forbidden Consumption is purely dark magic."

Kean waves his hand flippantly. "Others have faced the same darkness and prevailed. The great Doff ate his enemy's heart to gain his powers of insight and vision to defeat the Tulion sorcerers' clan. Cragon achieved a similar feat. They both survived unchanged."

"That is true, but…" Ryland pauses, taking in Kean's wide, crazed stare. He sits back and leans his elbows on the arms rests, interlocking his fingers as he chooses his words carefully. "Kordoff and Craigon were men of honor and virtue, qualities necessary to fight against the pull of dark magic."

Kean leans forward and slowly rises from his chair, glowering down at Ryland. "Are you saying that I'm not a man of honor and virtue?"

Ryland opens his mouth, but before he says anything he reaches for his drink and takes one more sip. He swallows the gin in a loud gulp, and it burns his throat. "I don't define what makes a man of honor. Your actions and intentions define your honor and virtue. Deception, betrayal…" he glances back up at Kean, "these are not the actions of honorable men."

Kean raises his voice. "I intend to give my family back the power that was unjustly taken from us. My father was the firstborn of his family, first before Caderyn's father. He deserved the leadership by birthright."

"The Foreman Clan's leadership is selected by your clan's magic. There is no birthright. Nothing was taken from your father."

Kean sneers. "Caderyn doesn't deserve it. Look what he's done with our clan. I'll restore greatness to the Foreman Clan, recover its dignity and glory, and erase the last few centuries of Caderyn's ineptitude from history. Are my intentions not honorable and virtuous?"

Ryland lowers his gaze to the floor. "Again, I do not define what is honorable or virtuous. If these are your truest intentions—"

"They are."

"Then I don't doubt that you will overcome the temptation of darkness should you perform the Forbidden Consumption." Ryland glances up at Kean for a second and then lowers his gaze once more.

Kean picks up his drink and finishes it in one long sip, and then places the glass on the table. He sits back down, wiping his lips with the back of his fingers, and glowers at Ryland.

"Darkness," Ryland says in an even tone, without looking at Kean, "isn't so much a captor as it is a deceiver, a seducer. If you're weak in your constitution, you won't have the inner strength to ward it off. You'll run to it and embrace it the way a man in the desert runs to a mirage and drinks the sand believing it's fresh water. That's when it consumes you, and you're no longer yourself."

A metallic squeal and a loud *thud* echoes through the chamber as the upper-level door opens and slams shut. A man in his early twenties wearing a gray rain jacket runs down the staircase and straight to Ryland's side. He whispers in his ear, and Ryland whispers back.

When the man dashes back up the stairs, Ryland leans forward to pour himself another glass. "Let us discuss the dragon."

Kean nods. "Do you know how to release it from its prison?"

"The Forbidden Consumption will do the trick. However, if you are unable to perform the Forbidden Consumption, there is another way. You will need Jasmyn's blood and a spell I found in the *Book of Sol*. It states—"

"You have the *Book of Sol*?" Kean sits upright. "I thought it was lost to the dragons' fire."

"No. I've had it for quite some time. Caderyn was aware of it." Ryland clears his throat. "The book states that entrapment spells can be broken with the original caster's blood. The captive is released immediately."

"The dragon will return to its normal size?"

"Yes, and at full strength. And you will be his master. However," Ryland gestures toward Kean, "nothing guarantees loyalty."

Kean narrows his eyes at Ryland. "Careful, Ryland. You tread heavily on volatile waters."

"My apologies." He presses his right hand flat against his chest. "It was meant as a warning, not a critique."

Kean fills his glass and lifts it to his mouth for a sip. "Can you make yourself scarce so Caderyn does not meet with you tomorrow? I want to keep him in the dark as long as possible. I'll invent an excuse for my absence."

"There's no need for that."

"What do you mean?"

"Caderyn is no longer here. He's left for the states."

Kean's head jerks back. "What?"

The right corner of Ryland's lip twists slightly upwards. "Miller, my young assistant, has just informed me that Caderyn arranged a private jet to the states."

Kean stands, his gaze following the staircase where Miller retreated and then back to Ryland. "Why would he leave? We planned to bring the case here and release the dragon."

Ryland sits quietly with a smug look on his face.

In one swift motion, Kean grabs Ryland by the neck, lifts him off the chair, and raises him high above the ground.

"You dare withhold information from me!"

"Do it." Ryland gags. "Kill me... and you will never... know... anything... more..."

Kean releases his grip, dropping Ryland to the ground, and steps away to adjust his suit sleeve. He scowls down at Ryland on the floor.

Ryland's throat scrapes with every cough. He spits several times before pushing himself to his hands and knees.

You can't kill me. You need me. You need my knowledge. Knowledge is my power.

Rubbing his throat and the back of his neck, Ryland rises to his feet. He returns Kean's scowl and clears his throat once more. "What amazes me is that you haven't yet figured out that Caderyn is undergoing the transfer."

Kean's eyes widen. His chest rises with a deep inhalation.

Ryland's scowl is almost a grin now. "Logan is his chosen heir."

Kean whips his arms upward, and all four chairs fly backward and crash against the far walls. When Kean releases a roar, the center table flattens with a single pound that reverberates across the floor and to the city streets outside.

Ryland stumbles backward and breathes heavily as Kean glares down at him. The loud *thud* of the chamber's door echoes, and Miller rushes down the spiral staircase straight to his master's side. Oregon shuffles in from a bedroom at the back of the chamber as fast as his elderly feet allow and gasps at the mess in the room.

Oregon manages to tie his robe before finally reaching Ryland. "Are you alright, my lord?"

Kean glowers at the two men at Ryland's side. "Your lord has defied me, and now," he locks his gaze upon Ryland, "one of you will suffer."

The strength Ryland felt moments ago now sinks out of his body. He stares straight into Kean's psychotic gaze as his body shivers with fear. He holds his breath as Kean lifts his right hand and whispers a spell through clenched teeth.

Miller goes floating into the air above him.

"I may need you alive, Ryland, but you will suffer a fate worse than death if you ever defy me again."

The sound of Miller's scream echoes in the chamber as Kean forms a claw with his right hand before closing it into a fist. His motions contort Miller's body, bending and twisting it as each finger curls inward, his skull crackling and veins exploding with each painful gasp of breath. Miller's screams are drowned by his own blood as his muscles, organs, and bones are mashed into drips of flesh and blood that fall into a large puddle of black and red muck.

With his mouth ajar, unable to utter even a sound of grief, and his eyes brimming with tears, Ryland gawks at Miller's remains. Miller, who worked for him only a year—is now gone. His death, the result of Ryland's foolish arrogance.

Paralyzed with emotion and terror, Ryland watches helplessly as Oregon wails in utter misery. Oregon had adopted Miller in his heart like a son. Self-loathing fills Ryland's heart at the horror of Miller's death. Yet, he feels a guilty relief that Kean chose Miller instead of Oregon to kill so gruesomely.

With his body completely stiff with shock, Ryland stares at what is left of Miller and speaks in a hoarse voice. "Forgive me, Kean." His bottom lip trembles. "It will never happen again."

13

ABSOLUTION

The cool evening breeze brushes Jasmyn's cheeks when she steps onto the terrace of the second-floor apartment. As she gazes at the million stars twinkling in the twilight sky, Jasmyn feels insignificant, unimportant, a non-vital piece of a vast universe. She can't interrupt the dynamics of the galaxies, can't touch the ocean of stars above her. Her existence has no effect on the cosmos, and she is momentarily thankful for that one truth.

But, when her gaze lowers to her hands resting on the metal rail, she's hit with fresh force by the knowledge that her very existence is the cause of the mess here below. If she hadn't started the chain of events that led to the release of the dragons, the news would never have reported the location of her grandmother's family, and Caderyn would never have seen his great-grandson. She is the reason Katarina is dead, and now she is the reason Logan's life is in danger.

Jasmyn closes her eyes once more and concentrates on the howling wind, searching for the calmness that eludes her. When the wind stops, she glances back through the patio's glass door and studies Arsen and Patricia conversing in the kitchen. Their faces are wrinkled with worry, their arms crossed tightly against their chests, shaking their heads as if every idea is unsatisfactory.

If two powerful sorcerers can't fix this, how can I? I don't even have my grandmother's memories or training in her magic abilities. How am I supposed to know how to turn back time? How am I supposed to erase everything that's happened? And now, Logan...

Jasmyn presses her eyelids shut as a new mountain of dread brews inside of her.

If Kean succeeds, Mom and Dad will...

She shakes her head at thought of her mother and father mourning the deaths of all their children, of their future.

As these thoughts rattle Jasmyn's core, the image of Katarina's bruised and bloodied face appears in her mind; the sound of her weak voice, begging for her mother, echoes in Jasmyn's ears. She grabs the metal handrail at the terrace's border and wrings it, flexing her forearms as her fingers twist around the edge. She screams up to the night in a cry so loud that it burns her throat. Out of breath, her roar diminishes and she inhales a lungful of air.

"No more!" she shouts at the stars, angry at their mocking tranquility. "No more." She hears her sister's voice crying out for their mother. "Please," she whispers, "please, no more."

Her shoulders fall forward as she leans her head on her hands against the metal handrail and whimpers. The patio door slides open behind her. When Patricia walks out, Jasmyn stands tall, straightens her T-shirt, and wipes her face dry.

"I want to be alone."

"Right, to punish yourself," Patricia says as she shuts the patio door.

Jasmyn closes her eyes and takes a deep breath. When she opens her eyes, Patricia is standing next to her, staring out into the desert night.

"I know you suffer in silence."

Jasmyn gazes further out into the abyss.

"I know you blame yourself for everything. I know you feel pain and anger and frustration and a load of other emotions. But, you have to use your pain to learn your grandmother's magic. Don't succumb to guilt. Take your pain, mold it into a purpose, and you will heal yourself of it."

"To what purpose?"

"To learning Agatha's magic. To learning the time-reversal spell so we can undo everything that has occurred. Keep going through all the magic you know, everything you've read in the *Book of Whispers*. Keep at it. It may trigger something inside of you."

"It hasn't triggered anything yet!" Jasmyn points out toward the night sky. "I've been in the desert all day executing elemental spells and using Brian as a guinea pig for controlling spells—and nothing. Nothing has been 'revealed' to me. Nothing new has 'occurred.' No new memories. No new magic. Nothing! And Katarina still won't talk to me in my dreams, and I'm just…"

Jasmyn swallows back a cry and takes a moment to smooth the tension on her face.

"Think of Katarina. If she were here and you had died, what would you want for her? Would you have wanted her to punish herself?"

"No… but I can't help the way I feel. Kat didn't have a mean bone in her body. She would never have treated me the way I treated her. She wouldn't have this… this…"

"Self-pity? Self-degradation? Guilt? Excuses?"

Jasmyn clenches her teeth. "You don't know what I feel."

Patricia frowns and plants her hands on her hips. "Do you think I don't know what it feels like to lose a sister? To watch my sister die in my arms because I wasn't fast enough or strong enough to save her? I've lost many sisters, both coven sisters and blood-related. Believe me, Jasmyn, I know *exactly* how you feel."

Jasmyn shakes her head. "You didn't torment your sisters or make them suffer! You weren't the cause of the events that led to their deaths!"

"No, that was Finna. If you want to blame someone with the obliteration of our clan, blame Finna. Her actions led to a chain of events that resulted in the coven's annihilation. Or blame Agatha for keeping secrets—secrets that led to you and your sister releasing the dragons. And if either of them had fallen into the same pity pool that you're swimming in, with the same self-blaming anchor you're holding onto, then none of us would be here today!"

Patricia's index finger shoots straight out at Jasmyn's chest. "You, Jasmyn, have decided to sink, and you will bring everyone down with you if you don't let go of that anchor and swim!"

Jasmyn stands frozen, staring with her mouth slightly open.

Patricia straightens but doesn't break eye contact. "Although Finna's betrayal triggered the war with the Foreman Clan, I don't blame her for their attack. Even though it was her idea to spawn the Gregorn Dragons, no one blamed her for the dragon rebellion. Yes, you tormented your sister; you hurt her in many ways, but you recognized your fault before the end. She knew it. She felt your love for her, and she left this world knowing that her one and only sister truly loves her."

"But—"

Patricia holds up her hand to stop Jasmyn from speaking. "Every single one of our actions has a long trail of consequences over which we have no control. If Baronyx had not attacked the helicopter, or if Katarina had not unbuckled herself, or if I had

102

reacted more quickly when she fell..." Patricia's eyes well up with tears that she blinks back. "Then, maybe, Katarina would be here with us right now. You had no say in what happened. You didn't control it. And no one, not any one of us, blames you for Katarina's death."

Tears stream down Jasmyn's cheeks.

"Say it."

Jasmyn stares at Patricia and blinks twice. "Say what?"

"Say, 'I'm not the reason Katarina is gone.'"

Jasmyn wipes her face dry and then inhales and exhales unsteadily. "I'm not the reason Kat..." She fights the grimace that threatens to choke off her voice.

"Say it."

"I'm not the reason Kat—" she gasps, "is gone."

"Say it one more time."

After closing her eyes for a few seconds, Jasmyn straightens her back and lifts her chin. "I'm not the reason Kat is gone."

When she opens her eyes, Jasmyn notices Patricia is holding both her hands. At that moment, Jasmyn realizes she heard Patricia's voice in unison with hers. Not once did she consider that Patricia blamed herself for Katarina's death. Not once did she see Patricia fight back a grimace or press her lips together to hold back a sob, until now.

As Patricia wipes a tear streaming down her cheek, Jasmyn grasps how much they both needed absolution. They needed to forgive themselves and accept forgiveness from each other. The guilt-drenched sorrow buried deep in Jasmyn's heart lifts off her body and into the air like smoke rising from cooling embers. The warm, peaceful vibrations emanating from Patricia's aura calm Jasmyn into believing her words, their words. And for the first time since Katarina's death, Jasmyn can breathe normally.

~ ~ ~

Jasmyn opens the terrace door and walks in to join Brian on the couch. Gustavo sees Patricia standing on the terrace alone, looking out into the night. He heads for the door and slides it open.

"Major Brigante was able to get us a flight to New York. It leaves in two hours."

Patricia turns around to face him as she sucks in a lungful of air.

Gustavo lowers his voice. "Is everything okay? I saw you pointing your finger at Jasmyn as if you were accusing her of something."

Patricia lowers her gaze to the floor.

"What did you say to her?" Gustavo asks.

"Only what she needed to hear."

14

FOLLOWING ORDERS

Granger's lips twist in disgust, and a glob of saliva collects in his mouth as he watches the black and white monitor. He emits a low grunt and spits to the side as Arsen and Patricia appear on the screen standing on a porch talking with animated expressions. A young man steps out onto the porch and exchanges a few words with Arsen before returning inside the building. Granger narrows his eyes when Arsen leans in toward Patricia as if sharing a secret.

Kean was right about you, Arsen. Patricia has bewitched you.

Christopher, a stick-figure of a man who has worked the security console for the apartment complexes on NAS Fallon for the last five years, leans his pointy shoulders in toward a monitor and squints. He mutes his headset and turns to Granger. "A Humvee is arriving at the front door right now to take them to Reno Airport."

The outer angle of Granger's right eyebrow shoots upwards. "All of them?"

"It appears to be for all of them. An aircraft is being prepared to take them to New York City. The flight leaves in less than two hours."

Granger paces and rubs his wiry black beard. "Are they taking anything with them?"

Christopher pauses, cocking his head to listen more closely into his headset. "There is an order to move boxes from their room into a secure storage facility. We can intercept that transport." He swallows before speaking again. "I know where the facility is located. My car is right outside."

Granger smirks with self-satisfaction at his new servant. "Very good, Christopher. Your loyalty will be rewarded."

With sweat beading down his back, Christopher glances at the two dead bodies sprawled out on the floor beside him. His coworkers' necks were twisted until they snapped, leaving them as lifeless as rag dolls. Christopher glances back at Granger and clears his throat. "Thank you, sir."

He rises from his chair and leads Granger down the hallway, tiptoeing over the dead bodies of more coworkers that Granger encountered when first entering the third floor of the security building. When he reaches outside, he stops in front of a corpse torn in half through its midsection. He turns to the side to throw up.

"Just continue being of service, Christopher, and you'll remain in one piece."

~ ~ ~

Kean's voice sounds stern over the cellphone. "Do you have the dragon's entrapment case?"

"It's within reach. I'll have it soon and be on the next flight to Manchester."

"No. Don't go to Manchester. I'm headed to the states."

Granger stops in mid-stride and lifts his right hand. Christopher freezes in place. "Has something happened?" Granger asks.

"Yes. It seems Caderyn's successor has been chosen."

A long sigh escapes Granger. He closes his eyes and rubs his forehead as he recalls his lifetime with Caderyn, a friendship that stemmed from their youth. The thought of his passing saddens him.

Granger's face tenses into a scowl at the memory of Caderyn's actions that led to the destruction of their clan, and his inaction afterward which has reduced the clan to a fraction of what it once was. He rolls his shoulders and rubs at his beard. "Who's is it?"

"Agatha's grandson, Logan. He's Jasmyn's brother."

Granger recalls the image on the monitor and jerks his head back. "That teenage boy with Patricia and Arsen?"

"Have you seen him?"

"He's with them right now."

Kean huffs over the call. "I can't believe Arsen is still with them. Had I known he would run into Patricia, I would have sent you to get the relic."

"Where is Caderyn now?"

Silence hovers in the air for a few seconds. "He's gone into hiding."

"Hiding?" Granger snorts. "Caderyn wouldn't hide. He'd take action."

Kean releases a loud deep sigh.

Granger frowns. "What are you planning, Kean?"

Silence.

With his lips curled into a sideways smile, Granger shakes his head. "You are going to kill Caderyn, aren't you? You conniving worm. You're plotting against him."

"I'm doing no such thing."

"Arsen was right; you can't be trusted."

"You believe Arsen over me? That traitor has joined Finna's coven and is helping the same sorceress who decimated our people. And now Logan, Caderyn's heir is trying to convince Arsen to help the coven as well. Don't be a fool, Granger. I could have killed Caderyn the moment the transfer started, but I didn't, because I don't want that."

Granger huffs and rolls his eye. "Wasn't this your plan all along, introducing Caderyn to easy women who would bear him children and trigger the transfer of power? That was your only clear opportunity to take over the clan."

"And when the opportunity presented itself, I didn't take it? Is that not proof enough of my word?"

With his eyebrows in a stiff furrow, Granger considers Kean's argument.

Kean guffaws. "I find it amusing that you judge me when you yourself have betrayed Caderyn. Do you forget how vigorously you fought to nullify his marriage to Finna?"

"I was acting on behalf of the clan."

"Indeed. One could conclude that you are the cause of all our misery. If it weren't for your campaign, perhaps the council wouldn't have pushed for the annulment that forced Finna to flee."

"Her actions proved me right. She stole the dragon eggs. She should never have been trusted." A sourness fills Granger's mouth at the surge of memories. He spits to the side and huffs into the phone. "In any case, I apologized to Caderyn after the war, for attacking him the way I did. I didn't mean to question his character. I was merely trying to rid us of that woman. And he forgave me because he understood that I desired only the good of the clan."

"He still exiled you, did he not?"

"It no longer matters. I've never betrayed him again. You, however, are still plotting his death."

"I'm doing no such thing!"

Kean releases an exasperated sigh. He takes a moment before continuing in a calmer tone. "I understand your suspicion.

Back then, I was lost, selfish, driven by hatred. But now, Caderyn has a solid, trustworthy plan. The dragon will reignite our clan's destiny. We owe it to Caderyn to help restore his power and let him lead us to greatness."

Granger grumbles.

"*You* owe it to him. He could have killed you, and he didn't."

A moment passes as Granger ponders Kean's claim. "What is your plan then?

"To stop the transfer so Caderyn can regain his full strength."

Granger narrows his eyes. "You want to help Caderyn stop the transfer?"

"Yes. Regardless of what you may think of my past actions, my intent has always been to enhance the greatness of the Foreman Clan."

"Ah, yes," Granger's voice changes to a whisper, "the greatness of the Foreman Clan." A slew of memories rushes into Granger's mind like pent-up water breaking through a dam. The armies, the families, the land—Granger recalls when the Foreman Clan was one of the most powerful peoples in the world, one of the most respected, the most feared. His chest swells with pride of their past, and his heart grows heavy with melancholy. "We haven't seen greatness in centuries."

Kean's voice is deep and resonant. "Which is why I'm committed to seeing Caderyn's plan through. Arsen has betrayed us, and our ancestors; he wants to help Logan take Caderyn's power and join Patricia and her coven. Logan wasn't raised a Foreman, and he knows nothing of our clan, of our history. With the dragon in his possession, Caderyn can rebuild our clan's power. He needs us, his clan brothers, more than ever."

Granger's face twists into a warrior's snarl. "I won't let

Caderyn down. He can depend on me."

"Excellent. Get the relic, and bring Jasmyn alive—we need her blood to release the dragon. And don't kill Logan. Caderyn wants to kill Logan himself."

"Consider it done."

15

ANTICIPATION

Patricia stares deep into the eyes of the two soldiers who were assigned to move the boxes to the storage facility. She raises both her hands, closes her eyes, and whispers a protection spell.

"Just watch the boxes. Stay out of sight and as far away from the boxes as possible. If anyone tries to get to them, or if anything happens to them, call us. You don't have to save the boxes or fight off anyone trying to take them. Just let us know what happens. Do you understand?"

The two men nod in unison and proceed to the left to a brown Humvee. They drive down the road and turn out of sight.

"What was the spell for?" Gustavo opens the door as a passenger truck pulls up, ready to drive them to the airport.

Patricia climbs in. "A protection spell. Arsen suspects Kean has sent Granger after the dragon's entrapment case. Granger will destroy anything in his path. He cares little for the lives of anyone outside of his clan, far less the lives of mortals."

"What do you think he'll do when he finds out there's nothing in those boxes?"

A soldier closes the door behind Gustavo and opens the back door for Regina.

As she climbs inside the second row of seats, Regina scoffs. "Granger will be pissed off. He's got a mean temper. He likes slashing bodies, blood, gore." She sits down and releases a tired grunt.

"You don't have to come, Regina." Patricia says. "With me, Jasmyn, and Arsen, we have more than enough protection. You should stay and recuperate."

"Are you kidding me? And miss the transfer of power to a new Foreman Clan leader?"

Arsen takes off his suit jacket and steps inside the truck. He glances toward the front where Patricia and Gustavo sit and then proceeds to the third row.

"Besides," Regina continues as she watches Arsen take his seat, "I'm not sure I can trust Arsen yet."

"Ah… to win the trust of Regina I would need…" Arsen deduces bits of information from Regina's open aura. "Six-pack abs, a deep bass voice, and long, silky hair."

With her lips pursed and her arms folded, Regina faces forward. "Don't forget good manners," Regina adds in an aloof tone. "He has to be a gentleman."

"Right. A gentleman, if there ever was such a euphemism." After a few more seconds of reading her aura, Arsen asks, "Was Jacob a gentleman? No, wait… it's Armando now. Is Armando a gentleman? Or have you switched over to Walter?"

Regina shoots him a glare, lifts her arm and executes a spell that pushes him up against the right side of the truck with the seat belt wrapped tightly around his neck. Arsen chuckles, allowing her to feel a bit of power before drawing her magic back.

"Stop that!" Patricia glares at them both.

Regina releases her hold and rubs her throbbing right arm. She fights hard to maintain her composure despite the discomfort in her chest and stomach.

As Arsen unwraps the seat belt from his neck, he studies Regina for a second before recognizing her weakness. "Ah, I see.

Baronyx put a spell on you. Maybe you should stay and try to strengthen those muscles."

Regina rolls her eyes and stares out the window to her left.

"Leave her alone, Arsen," Patricia warns.

"Her aura is an open book." Arsen sits back in his seat with a huff of satisfaction. "I'm not doing anything but accepting the information she releases freely."

"Do we really need him?" Regina crosses her arms and legs. She glares at Arsen and rolls her eyes away.

"Yes." Patricia's voice is firm. "He's our connection to Caderyn. Until Logan and Caderyn have completed the transfer, Arsen is part of our team."

"And afterward?" Regina asks.

"Then he'll be part of Logan's clan."

Arsen smirks, and Regina releases an unsatisfied sigh.

~ ~ ~

"There's the truck." Christopher decelerates, keeping far behind the brown Humvee. He gulps hard as he listens to Granger whisper something under his breath. Granger holds his hand out in front of him and twists it.

The Humvee floats up into the air, turns upside down, and lands on its hood. It slides off the road to the right. Thick plumes of dirt and gravel follow its path until it comes to a full stop.

The truck's headlights flicker before Granger shatters the bulbs. The two soldiers in the truck struggle to climb out of the main cabin, but Granger raises his arms once more and renders them unconscious. Their bodies fall limply to the ground.

Christopher stops his car right behind the flipped

Humvee and jumps out. He runs to the back, opens the rear compartment door, and pulls out the first box.

With long, relaxed strides, Granger walks toward the driver side of the truck. He bends down to study the soldier lying on his belly with his head twisted at an awkward angle. "I didn't mean to kill you." He stands up and watches Christopher tearing through another box. "Not yet, at least."

He meets Christopher at the back of the truck. After discarding several small cases filled with colorful stones, cracked jars filled with herbs and other useless containers, Christopher tosses out the last box of artifacts.

"It's… it's not here." Christopher stares weakly at the desert floor, his lips trembling. "Most of these boxes are empty."

A snarl forms on Granger's lips before he releases a roar and flips the truck across the desert field about fifty feet away. He imagines the victorious looks on Arsen and Patricia's faces, and he squeezes his hands shut until the truck crumples into a ball of contorted metal parts, falling to the ground and then catching on fire.

Twisted necks, a split torso, inefficient decapitations… you will suffer, Arsen. I'll tear through you and your lot, and I'll take my time. You will all suffer.

Granger hears a moan from the other soldier that was on the passenger side. With the sneer planted solidly on his face, he marches over to the young man twisting in pain on the ground. He gets down on one knee. "Are you in pain, soldier?"

"My legs," he cries out, his face in agony.

Granger sees his two legs bent backward at the knees. "That looks horrible. You must be in terrible pain."

The soldier nods frantically.

"Let me show you what real pain feels like."

The soldier opens his eyes wide as Granger rises with his

hands in fists. He lifts the soldier up from the ground and holds him suspended in midair. "There is no pain equivalent to the fear of knowing you're about to die."

"No. No—"

With a flick of his wrist, Granger sends the soldier flying straight into the center of the bonfire.

He shoots a glare at Christopher, who stands frozen, with his mouth agape and his entire body trembling with fear. "If you value the blood coursing through your veins, you will get me to the airport before their plane departs."

Without hesitation, Christopher runs back to the car and starts the engine. When Granger slams the passenger door shut, Christopher floors the accelerator.

~ ~ ~

As the escort truck drives to the airport, the constant rhythm of pebbles bouncing against the underside of the vehicle lulls Jasmyn into drowsiness. She yawns and leans her head against Brian's shoulder.

"You know," she whispers, "if we succeed, you won't remember any of this happened. In fact, it won't have happened to you at all. Only a memory of all of this will remain in my head."

Brian chuckles and reaches for Jasmyn's hand. "Promise me you'll look for me after you go back."

"I'll try."

"What do you mean, 'I'll try.' You know exactly where I live. You know where to find me."

"But, you'll be different."

"Me? How?"

She pulls away to face him. "You're going through this

with me right now. You know why I am the way I am, and you know how much I've changed. You've been by my side through so much, and we've bonded because of that. So, what if…"

He raises an eyebrow. "If?"

"What if you hate me. What if you find out how horrible I was to my little sister and everyone else and…"

Jasmyn pulls back further and looks away.

"I won't hate you. You're not that jealous person anymore, right? You're different now."

"But my family will be the same. They'll know the past me, and I was… horrible. I was a horrible, horrible person."

"I'm sure you weren't that bad."

Jasmyn shivers. "I was jealous of Kat and treated her horribly. I mean, I was a horrible sister. Just horrible. It breaks my heart just thinking about it."

"Okay, first things first, when you get back, get a thesaurus because your vocabulary sucks."

Jasmyn chuckles as she wipes a tear from the corner of her eye.

"And second, don't you control how far back you go? Maybe you can go further back in time and not do the things you did—or do them differently. Think about the last time you and your sister were on good terms, and go back then. Knowing what you know now, things will surely be different."

A deep breath fills Jasmyn's lungs, and she exhales as she ponders the last time she and Katarina were happy together. Her chest grows tight, and her eyes fill with tears as she realizes how many years back that was.

"And third, when you find me, you'll have to tell me everything."

"Are you kidding? You'll think I'm crazy."

"Not if you tell me something I know no one else in the

world would know, and the only way that you would know is if I told you."

"Is there a deep, dark secret you can share with me that would fit that description?"

Brian raises his eyebrows, and a hint of a smile crosses Jasmyn's face. He rolls his eyes to the side. "When you moved out of the neighborhood, I wrote you a ton of letters."

"You did?" The smile on Jasmyn's face grows to full length.

"I wrote at least two dozen letters, but I never sent them. I chickened out."

The red in her face matches Brian's blush, and it makes Jasmyn look away. She feels a rush of heat from sitting so close to him. "What did you write?" she whispers.

"Stuff," he says in a playful tone.

Jasmyn nudges Brian's arm, lifts it up, and wraps it around her shoulder. She snuggles into his hold further as he squeezes his arm around her frame. The past few days she's fought off the warm vibrations emanating from Brian's aura, but now, Jasmyn embraces his warmth. She inhales a whiff of his scent, and her mind runs away with thoughts of kissing him.

"Where are these letters?" she asks in a whisper. Her eyes follow the curvature of his lips.

"In my apartment. In a box with other old keepsakes in the back of my closet."

"Describe the box?"

"A green shoe box, lots of photos inside, some birthday cards."

"Any other love letters?"

Brian chuckles to the side.

"You will definitely think I'm crazy. So, the more details I have, the better my chances of convincing you I'm sane."

"You forget that I knew you when you used to wear that football helmet as part of your space suit. You were always a little loopy."

"Loopy?" Jasmyn sits up and stares down at Brian. "I like to think I was an eccentric kid."

He smiles and blinks lazily. "Just promise me you'll look for me."

She buries her head in Brian's shoulder once more. "Okay. I promise."

16

IDENTITIES

War horns blare far away at the foot of a mountain. Once they stop, Caderyn walks to the edge of the cliff to look down toward the shoreline, pressing his fist against the stab wound at his side. He steps away from the edge and sits on a rock.

Granger glides a smooth gray stone across the length of his sword's blade. "It's a good day to fight."

Kean and Arsen both follow the circular edges of the summit, examining the shores surrounding the island.

"I told you we should have brought more men." Kean spits over the edge toward the army.

Caderyn looks up from his wound. "This was a wedding, a celebration. If I had thought they were a threat—"

"Everyone is a threat!" Kean steps right in front of Caderyn, pointing to the ground. He shouts close to Caderyn's face. "I've told you time and again—we can't trust anyone!"

Granger pauses his work and stands, glaring at Kean. Arsen also turns around and glares at Kean. Caderyn lifts his arm, gesturing for both men to stand down.

"You're right. We can't trust anyone. Not anymore."

Kean nods, glances at both Arsen and Granger, and then steps back and away from Caderyn toward the cliff's edge. Arsen turns around and resumes surveying their enemy's battle formations. Granger resumes sharpening his sword.

The sting of the stab wound spreads along Caderyn's side. He rips another strip of cloth from his shirt to press against

119

his stab wound as he continues to attempt healing spells. They're not working. Although he drank only a sip of the enchanted wine at the dinner, all of his powers have been affected.

The men at the base of the mountain bang on their drums and begin a menacing chant. They shoot fiery arrows toward the summit, but they fall short. The chanting stops with a final drum beat, and the morning sky is once again calm and quiet.

"I can't see their strategy." Arsen shakes his head. "I can't conduct any spells."

Granger stabs his sword into the ground. "We'll have to kill them the old-fashioned way." He picks up a battle ax and inspects the blades. "One split-open head at a time."

Arsen turns to face Granger. "The four of us can't fight that many men. There are at least five hundred down there."

"Five hundred cowards." Kean spits over the edge once more.

Arsen rolls his eyes. "I don't think they care what we label them."

"Or about having a fair fight. The herb they put in our wine… only a slithering worm would cast a spell that way."

"If you could blunt your enemy's weapon, you'd do so as well. An army of five hundred men is no match for our magic, and they probably knew that."

Granger mumbles, "That's what we get for drinking cheap wine."

"We should have known better." Caderyn stands and stretches his side.

"How were we to know they'd betray us?" Arsen asks.

"I meant about the wine." Caderyn grunts and then looks Arsen straight in the face. "These are Tulions. They *only* know how to make cheap wine."

Arsen smiles and chuckles first, and then Kean and

Granger follow.

Caderyn sighs. Tensions are high, and anything that eases the strain will benefit them in battle.

Arsen digs into his sack and pulls out a small bottle. He pops the cork. "Only the finest grain spirits for us."

Arsen takes a swig from the bottle and hands it to Kean. Kean lifts the bottle high, swallows the liquor, and gasps from the burn in his throat. He passes it over to Granger.

"The drink of honorable warriors." Granger guzzles down his share and releases a loud sigh of satisfaction. He hands the bottle to Caderyn.

Caderyn holds the bottle down at his side and stands before the three men. He straightens his back in spite of the throbbing pain in his side and gives each of them a stern look. He inhales a shaky breath, holds it as the pain stings deeper, and then blows it out steadily.

"We lost two brothers today, Brin and Rogen."

The men all bow their heads in respect.

"They sacrificed themselves so we could flee. I did not command them to do so. It was their choice. And for this," he raises the bottle, "I drink to them. I owe them my life. We owe them our lives. Let's not let their sacrifice go to waste."

The three men nod as Caderyn tips the bottle upside down and finishes the liquor. He drops the bottle and paces in a circle, balling his fists as he concentrates on his magic. Digging deep down inside, Caderyn calls upon his father's magic, and the magic of his ancestors, to fight the effects of the enchanted wine. He repeats a single spell over and over, spitting the words out of his mouth, pressing his fists tighter with each iteration.

Arsen, Granger, and Kean all chant the same spell for Caderyn. The three men fall to one knee as they use all their strength to call upon their ancestors to help Caderyn rid himself of the poison. When the men see Caderyn's aura glow a dull yellow, they chant louder, pressing harder. All four men recite the spell using all their might until a small earthquake shakes the mountain and gray storm clouds materialize high in the sky.

Caderyn stands tall as the pain at his side dissipates. The wine and all its contents, all its enchantment, have vanished from his body. His aura is glowing a deep, dark royal blue, and the full power of his clan's magic now flows through his veins.

A roar forms in the pit of his stomach and bursts from Caderyn's mouth. He lifts his arms up, with his hands and fingers in a menacing claw formation, and slams them back down to his sides. A heavy gust of wind pours from the center of the summit and flows down along the mountainside toward the shoreline and out to the sea. The wind grazes the cheeks of every single man in the Tulion army, and Caderyn commands them all to kill the closest man.

Caderyn, Arsen, Kean, and Granger watch with utter satisfaction as the Tulion soldiers wipe themselves out.

~ ~ ~

Logan mindlessly follows the military detail through the airport as Caderyn's memory sinks in. The camaraderie he felt with his brothers in battle conflicts with current sentiments toward Kean. He stares at the ground as he follows the soldier, with his hands in his pockets, contemplating the drastic differences between the past and now.

A grimace appears on his face. *No. I am not Caderyn. These are his memories, not mine.* He glances at Jasmyn. *Kean is trying to kill us. Focus!*

A breeze flows in through the security door as they exit the corridors out onto the open runway. As they walk towards their airplane, a growing sense of unease tugs at his core. Suddenly, a tremor shoots through his body and out toward the tips of his limbs. Jerking to a halt, Logan scans the airport runways, searching for danger.

Patricia and Arsen stop alongside him. Jasmyn doesn't notice Logan's hesitation and continues to the airplane beside Gustavo and Regina. Brian and Walter continue walking side by side, discussing different types of military aircraft. A soldier pushing a cart with their bags and boxes leads the group.

Logan spins to look behind. "He's here."

Patricia frowns. "Who's here?"

"Granger." Arsen looks around the vast runway. "He's near."

Logan furrows his eyebrows as he reads Granger's thoughts. "He's here to take me and Jasmyn hostage. Kean told him specifically *not* to kill me."

Arsen nods. "If he kills you, Caderyn will regain his full strength, and Kean won't have a chance to defeat him."

"Wait." Logan gasps and looks at Arsen with pleading eyes as Granger's plan of attack unravels in his mind.

Arsen sees it too and raises his hands to cast a spell that lifts Jasmyn, Gustavo, and Regina into the air and pulls them back toward himself. As if Arsen's spell had pulled a trigger, the airplane explodes, sending everyone flying backward.

A long, high-pitched tone rings in Logan's ears. The rumbling on the floor keeps him conscious, but he presses his eyes shut as he struggles to keep his head up. The ringing noise increases and muffles out more explosions. Another crash sounds directly overhead, and he covers his head with his hands.

As he blinks his eyes open, squinting through the smoke around him, the image of Katarina lying still in her coffin flashes in his mind. It quickly transforms into an image of Jasmyn in a coffin, and Logan's heart races.

Logan presses his eyes shut and shakes his head to erase the images. He mouths Jasmyn's name, unable to find his voice. He tries twice more, but nothing comes out. After rolling to his side, he pushes himself up to his hands and knees and looks around. "Jasmyn?" he whispers.

Through the haze, Logan sees a dark pillar of smoke rising from a roaring flame. He calls out for his sister once more, shouting as best he can while spitting dirt from his mouth.

Arsen arrives at Logan's side and helps him up to his feet.

"Where's Jasmyn?" Logan asks weakly. The ringing in his ears begins to lessen.

Arsen points to Jasmyn kneeling next to Regina. Together they tend to Brian and Walter who are lying unconscious.

Gustavo appears from behind Arsen. "We have to get out of here. Patricia can't hold the shield much longer."

A *thump* to his right catches Logan's attention. He turns to face a second *thump*, and another behind him. More and more thumping sounds fill the air alongside the sound of bullets ricocheting off the shield.

As the smoke clears, Logan sees the source of the muffled sounds. Horror sinks into the pit of his stomach as he sees airport workers running into the shield and bashing their heads against it. Each hit increases in force and continues until the workers bash their skulls so hard that they crack open, splattering Patricia's shield with thick red blood and brain tissue. Their lifeless bodies slide to the ground, making way for more workers to step up and bash their heads against the shield.

Arsen pulls Logan by the arm. "Don't look at them." He shakes Logan at the shoulders. "Look at me, Logan. Look at me!" He finally gets Logan's attention. "The only way we can help any of them is to stop Granger. Do you understand?"

Logan nods, still dazed. He concentrates on Arsen's intense stare.

An object in the air grabs Logan's attention. Just as Arsen turns around to see it, an airplane comes crashing down on Patricia's shield and explodes. Patricia screams as another plane hits. The second blast is so powerful that it knocks Patricia off her feet and she falls unconscious to the ground.

"The shield!" Regina lifts her arms in the air. Jasmyn joins her to strengthen their barrier.

Arsen runs to Patricia's side and exhales profoundly when he realizes she's still alive.

Jasmyn screams in terror at the top of her lungs as two workers bash their heads against her new shield.

"Don't look at them!" Arsen performs a spell to counteract Granger's enchantment, keeping him from reaching more people.

She closes her eyes and presses them tight. "I feel them! Their blood, their brains, on my skin." She screams again as more people attack. "I feel their skulls cracking!"

Arsen gives up his futile attempts at counteracting Granger's spell and joins Jasmyn and Regina, raising his arms straight up to reinforce the shield.

Hundreds more airport personnel run out onto the runway and head straight for them. A wave of pounding footsteps shakes the ground as a swarm of people race to the shield, all screaming at the top of their lungs. Arsen, Jasmyn, and Regina brace themselves as they feel the barrage of dozens of bodies pushing in against them, senselessly trampling each other, climbing over one another other as if they're desperate to ram their heads in.

Jasmyn cries weakly as the clear shield is covered in splattered flesh and blood. The war cries grow steadily as if more men have arrived. Her arms tremble from the pressure against the shield, from watching the gory deaths in front of her, from feeling blood and tissue dripping down her skin.

"Don't look at them, Jasmyn!" Regina's knees buckle. "Look away!"

Jasmyn closes her eyes as tightly as she can.

"Logan!" Arsen yells. "You're Caderyn's heir!"

Logan shakes his head and shrugs his shoulders. "I... don't..."

"Use his powers!" Arsen's arms weaken from the sheer volume of people attacking the shield. He grunts. "It's inside of you. Find it!"

Breathing heavily now, Logan scans the outside of the entire dome shield, lined with piles of dead bodies and mindless people bashing their heads in. Logan shuts his eyes and balls his fists as tightly as he can.

If there ever were a time to transfer magic, now is the goddamned time! How did you defeat the Tulion army? How did you control those people?

He inhales and exhales deeply, blocking out the noises around him, concentrating on the memories he's already inherited.

Come on, Caderyn. Come on!

17

BREAKING TIES

An electric sensation jolts through Logan's body as the magic from the memory transfers into his core. He closes his eyes and drops to his hands and knees, breathing heavy and clenching his jaw as his muscles burn with a strength he's never before felt.

When he opens his eyes, he sees Jasmyn, Regina and Arsen struggle to hold up their defense as Granger sends two more airplanes crashing down upon them. Regina falls to the ground and Arsen stands taller with his arms spread out. More victims ram their heads into the shield, and Jasmyn's knees tremble upon each impact.

As the battery of human sacrifices weakens the shield, Logan rises from his knees. He stands tall, inhales deeply, and, in a booming voice, he shouts, "Enough!"

Within seconds, everyone outside their shield drops to the ground as if their life source was pulled from their bodies. A broken airplane Granger shot their way freezes in midair and falls straight down. Logan's voice carries across the airport, and whatever hold Granger had on anyone is now gone.

As a relative tranquility falls upon the scene, Patricia awakens. Arsen helps her rise to her feet as he quickly explains what has occurred. Gustavo, Jasmyn and Regina run over to Brian and Walter who are still unconscious.

Logan hears the crackling sound of fire around him, and the *whoosh* of a gust of wind that pushes the smoke up and away.

Turning to the horizon, he searches for Granger's exact location. "Granger!" Logan shouts as he scans the open field. "You believe I'm not worthy to be Caderyn's successor. Come out and allow me to show you that I am."

"What are you doing?" Patricia whispers to Logan.

"I'm challenging him," he replies in a low voice just above a whisper.

Arsen shakes his head and grabs his arm. "You can't challenge him. You're not ready to go up against someone like Granger. You don't have that level of power yet."

"I know. I want him to address me so that I—" Logan feels the pull. "There. That way." He juts his chin outward. "He's thinking about my challenge. He's wondering how much of Caderyn's power I possess." Logan wrinkles his forehead. "He's keeping his distance. He's afraid I'll have control over him." He turns to Arsen. "Do I?"

"You might. As our clan leader, your word is our command."

"How?"

Arsen lifts his shoulders and shakes his head. "It's not something I can show you. It's something that you, as the clan leader, will simply know."

Logan sighs as more of Granger's thoughts trickled into his mind. "Kean's lied to him. He's tricked Granger into thinking Caderyn wants me dead. That's why he's attacking us."

"Kean would do something like that."

More information flows in. Logan sees Granger's fear of aligning with the coven, of being under Jasmyn's or Patricia's command, a degradation in Granger's mind. He shakes his head. "We have to talk to Granger. We have to explain—"

"Talk to him?" Patricia interrupts. "You have to kill him!"

Logan turns to Patricia. "It's not that simple."

"Why not? Granger means nothing to you."

"But he does. I... I feel their brotherhood. Granger and Caderyn have a long history together, and it's becoming my history."

Patricia steps in front of Logan. "Granger just tried to kill you and Jasmyn. You need to put this into perspective. You have to kill him."

Like a rising tide stirred up by a deep-sea earthquake, Logan's chest fills with indignation. He doesn't fight it. He doesn't question it. He accepts it as it is.

He stands up straight, taller than just seconds earlier, and steps toward Patricia.

She takes a step back.

In a voice stronger than ever before, a voice that is part Caderyn's and his ancestors, Logan says, "*You* do not tell *me* what to do with my clansmen."

Patricia's lips part, and she takes another step backward. After scanning Logan from head to toe, she returns his threatening stare.

Arsen steps between Patricia and Logan. "This is not the time to pound chests."

"Patricia!" Gustavo shouts, drawing everyone's attention. He has one hand pressed against Walter's neck and the other on Brian's. "Walter's not responding. Neither is Brian. I can't get a pulse on either of them."

"Please, Brian," Jasmyn whispers. "Don't..."

Regina and Arsen both kneel between the two men and whisper healing spells as they move their hands in circular motions over each man's body. After a few seconds, Regina's stops to rub her trembling hands. Arsen continues his incantation until his hands begin to shake.

"They're alive." He looks up at Gustavo. "We have to get them to the hospital." He grabs hold of Regina and helps her to her feet. "You should go too."

"No. I'm fine."

"You're weak, but you still have your healing powers. Brian and Walter need you, in case…"

She glances at Jasmyn and nods. "Right."

Patricia steps in front of Logan. "Granger is a raging beast. He won't stop until we're all dead."

"I'll handle him."

"Handle him? Are you going to kill him or not?"

"It's not that simple!" Logan shouts back.

Jasmyn ignores Logan, Patricia and Arsen as they argue about their next steps. Their voices fade into the background and mix with the constant hum of the fires around them. Jasmyn stares down at Brian and presses her lips together to keep them from trembling, swallowing hard and holding in the scream that's dying to burst out.

Then, she remembers Brian's last request, his voice echoing in her thoughts. *Promise me you'll look for me and tell me everything.*

His profound stare, the way he held her in his arms, and the way his aura caressed hers. Jasmyn closes her eyes for a brief moment recalling how his warm smile found a way to calm her anxiety. Now, its memory will ease her anxiety and give her strength.

I promise, Brian. Jasmyn stands and takes a deep breath. *When we are back before all this happens, I'll find you and tell you everything.*

Like unpredictable storm clouds transforming into a tornado, Jasmyn's fear and guilt morph into a need for vengeance. She wipes her face dry and charges toward Logan, interrupting his argument.

"Show me where he is. If you won't kill him, then I will."

"Jaz, don't."

She balls her fists. "You have no authority over me." Patricia stands right next to Jasmyn, and Jasmyn glances at her from the corner of her eye. "*You* cannot tell *us* what to do."

"He was staring out toward the south." Patricia points her chin outward. "That must be where Granger is."

Jasmyn charges past Logan and Arsen, and Patricia follows.

"Jasmyn," Logan shouts in a stern tone he's never used with her.

A bitter mixture of rage and sadness fills Jasmyn's eyes as she comes to a halt. She turns back around to look at her brother. Logan has never called her 'Jasmyn.' She's been 'Jaz' since he was three when he pronounced her name with a lisp so adorable that everyone in their family decided the lispy name was better than the original. She scowls at Logan and Arsen and presses her lips tight.

"I'm not at war with you."

"If you're not at war with us, then kill Granger. Didn't you see what he just did?"

Logan sighs and passes both his hands through his hair as he formulates his thoughts. Caderyn's brotherhood with Granger, a lifetime of memories with ancient families, his personal memories with his own family, his parents, and now an estranged sister… a whirlwind of old faces and recent events fills his mind, and he shakes his head to scatter them.

"Could you kill me so easily?"

Jasmyn narrows her eyes at his question.

A frown appears on his face, and his eyes turn red. He

turns to Patricia. "You and Nana had known each other for centuries, been through everything together. If she had turned against your family, could you kill her so easily?"

Patricia glances away.

He turns back to Jasmyn. "What if I said killing me would save Kat. Would it be easier to kill me then?"

Her lips part, and her chest aches at the thought of choosing one sibling over another. "That's not fair."

"No, it isn't."

He sighs and closes his eyes for a few seconds.

"Granger is my brother. That might mean nothing to you, but for me it means a lifetime of brotherhood, of friendship, of sacrifices." He shakes his head and glances down for a second. "I know what I must do, but remember, only *I* will live with the consequences, the guilt. Not you or anyone else. So I ask you again, would it be so easy for you to kill me?"

Jasmyn's gaze softens. "No."

"No, it wouldn't." He turns to Patricia. "In fact, you would probably try to reason with me, right?"

Patricia nods. She looks down and steps back.

"That's what I'm trying to do. I'm not your enemy, Jaz. Nor yours, Patricia. But don't think for a second that either of you controls me."

He looks back at Arsen once more before charging toward Granger.

"Get them to a hospital and find another plane." Arsen places his hand on Patricia's arm, stealing her attention away from Logan's departure. "When this is over, we'll find you."

~ ~ ~

As Logan marches toward Granger, he sees the gears

turning inside his brother's mind. He sees Granger personally dismembering Patricia and Regina, burning their body parts in a large fire as the others watch helplessly. Logan winces at his plans to capture and torture Jasmyn to the brink of death, keeping her alive just enough so Caderyn could take her heart.

He wishes Granger didn't have such disdain for the coven.

They come to a full stop at the edge of the runway where a stretch of dry land leads to rolling desert hills. He gazes out to the peaks touching the dusk sky along the horizon.

"He despises me and is warning me to stay back." Logan turns to Arsen. "What can I say to Granger to change his mind?"

"Try sharing some of your recent memories with him. Perhaps he'll see that you and I are not under Patricia or Jasmyn's control and that we are the ones truly working with Caderyn." Arsen nudges Logan's arm. "Let's see if you've inherited Caderyn's gift of persuasion."

Logan huffs. "Let's hope so."

After a few moments of intense concentration in order to share memories with Granger, Logan sighs and shakes his head. "He doesn't believe me."

A low rumble emanates from beneath Arsen's and Logan's feet, shaking the earth. With his hands raised in the air, Arsen plants a shield in front of Logan and pushes it back toward the mountain. A wave on the ground defines the shield's growing border.

Logan grabs Arsen's arm. "No. Don't attack him. Let me try again."

"Granger is a stubborn man, and one who hungers for the blood of his enemies."

"But I'm not his enemy. Kean's lied to him. He's acting on inaccurate information."

"That *is* unfortunate. But, you have to consider that he will never make amends with Finna's coven. And, he believes we're under their control. Although Caderyn gave him orders to bring you back alive, he might still plan to kill you."

Caderyn's memories of Granger's actions produce a heaviness in Logan's heart. He recalls how Granger became cold and distant once he learned of Caderyn's engagement to Finna, how he fervently advised against the union. Then Granger had openly charged Finna with bewitching Caderyn, and he'd accused her of using magic to enchant other men and women from the clan. He'd used his position to influence the elders and the council.

Logan shakes his head. "He wasn't always so calculated. I recall happier memories with him, with his parents, his younger siblings. He was once goodhearted."

"Yes, when we were boys growing into young men, naive and trusting, with no personal agendas or opinions." Arsen sighs as a few innocent memories dash across his mind. "We haven't been those young men in a very long time."

They resume their walk toward Granger as more memories appear in Logan's head. "There were so many opposing forces within the clan."

"As is the nature of men, I'm afraid. I don't believe mankind was designed to live in peace. If we had been, it would be easier to distinguish between right and wrong, good and bad. Instead, we have different beliefs between civilizations, opposing beliefs that lead to disruption and war. No one is right, and no one is wrong."

Logan huffs and nods.

"Even within our own clan, we struggled to define peace. What was right for you, marrying Finna, was not right for Granger. Peace for you brought him rage. You were once brothers, and now you're enemies, both claiming to be in the right."

"What makes it all worse are the good memories. If we could only forget the good memories, the bad ones would be easier to accept."

"Ah," Arsen smirks. "Nostalgia is an unreliable friend. Those same youthful memories were the reason Caderyn spared Granger's life. He exiled him when he should have killed him for his betrayal. We all ceased communication."

"Except for Kean, apparently." Logan stops as a thought strikes, and he spins to face Arsen. "Did you know Kean maintained contact with him?"

"I did." Arsen releases a loud exhale.

Logan narrows his eyes as he waits for an explanation.

"I'm caught in the middle, trying to keep relative peace amongst the few brothers I have left in this world. I didn't choose to be in this position."

"Do you still think peace is an option for us now?"

Arsen gazes out to the horizon and turns back to Logan. "Caderyn wanted peace. He didn't kill Granger because he didn't want to be *that* kind of leader."

"And what kind of leader is that?"

"The kind that eliminates all opposing thoughts. He wanted his clan to have the freedom of ideas, to discuss their ideas openly and come to a resolution through careful thought and debate."

"But Granger's actions started a war."

Arsen sighs. "We know that now, in hindsight. At the time, he was just opposed to his union with Finna, as were so many other clansmen. But, ultimately Caderyn made his own decisions. He was torn between two people, and no matter how much Finna and Caderyn both wanted peace, the clan pressured them into choosing otherwise."

Logan shakes his head.

"At the end of the war," Arsen says in a quiet voice, "we all blamed Caderyn. His decisions, his actions, took us along a path that eventually led to our clan's destruction. But, I've spent many decades wandering the Earth, and in that time, I've contemplated millions of courses of actions that could have led to different outcomes. After learning how Finna turned back time to change the course of history, I realized that we are all at the mercy of the unpredictability of the universe."

Arsen gazes back out toward the horizon. "The first time around, we almost wiped out the coven. The second time around, they wiped us out, but then the dragons betrayed them. What will happen if Kean succeeds and we have a third chance? Will the dragons take over completely? Will there be another clan who will use the knowledge of all possible histories and dominate us all? Who knows? You, me, Finna, Caderyn… we're all pawns in the grand game."

"And who is playing this game? Who has control over us all?"

"No one has control, and at the same time we all have control." Arsen shrugs his shoulders. "That's both the horror and the beauty of it."

A thick gust of wind kicks up dirt in front of Logan, and they both look toward the hills where Granger awaits. Logan turns back toward the airport. He sees the wreckage of the airplanes Granger sent their way, next to the tall pile of dead bodies. The fires still burn as the last glimmers of orange sunlight set behind the western horizon.

Arsen turns back and stares out in the same direction. "You asked me if I think peace is an option."

Logan faces Arsen.

136

"Caderyn was Granger's clan brother since infancy; yet, Caderyn was unable to convince Granger to make peace with the coven. I doubt you will have any influence on him." Arsen shakes his head. "I don't think peace is an option anymore. Say the word, and I'll execute the order."

"No." Logan looks back out toward the hills. "Granger must die, but if I'm giving the order, then I will execute it."

18

FALLEN

A twisting knot in the pit of Caderyn's stomach awakens him from his deep sleep. He bends forward, clutching the lapel of his suit with his right hand and wringing the luxurious fabric into his chest. With his face in an agonized twist, he pushes his left forearm into his stomach and presses his forehead against the seat in the next row.

"Granger." He grinds his teeth. "You were always so stubborn."

He sees images of giant boulders the size of an eighteen-wheel truck crushing down on Granger while the ground below his feet crumbles. Logan and Arsen slam Granger's body from side to side. Logan sends bolts of lightning from a hovering cloud down to strike Granger in his torso. Enormous balls of rubble rise from the ground and rain down on Arsen and Logan in a counterattack. The battle scene unfolds crisply in Caderyn's mind.

He sees the exhausted looks in Arsen and Logan's faces as they stand over Granger's beaten body explaining the truth, and then the pain in Logan's eyes when Granger spits in his face and calls them both betrayers of the Foreman Clan.

Logan pleads with Granger, trying to reason with him, attempting to expose Kean's lies, but Granger launches himself at Logan with full force. He intends to kill or be killed. Caderyn feels Logan's hesitation when he lifts his hands and slams Granger down onto the ground one last time, and he shakes his head as he feels the pain in Logan's heart when he raises his hand for the final deadly strike.

Logan decapitates Granger, then falls to his knees in agony.

Through his brotherhood's magic, Caderyn feels everything his brothers feel. He recalls how the first few deaths he experienced were debilitating, sometimes leaving him unconscious, just as Granger's death has now left Logan shaking with seizures.

Then, the engulfing pitch-dark that follows a brother's death—a glimpse of the fate they will all, one day, meet.

An excruciating howl hovers at the tip of Caderyn's tongue as Granger's final thoughts and pain pass, but he manages to stifle it. After losing hundreds of his brothers in many wars, Caderyn has developed a tolerance for such pain.

Several minutes pass as Caderyn works at regaining control of his breathing. He finally opens his eyes to the present and finds a beautiful woman staring down at him.

"Are you feeling alright, sir?" The flight attendant asks.

With his finger placed upon his lips, Caderyn signals the flight attendant to whisper so as not to wake the little girl sleeping in the seat next to him. When she boarded, her long, auburn hair captured his full attention, and the information flowed automatically into his mind—only ten years old and traveling alone. The little girl shuffles under her blue cover, and her pink name tag with "Sasha" written on its front pokes out over the edge of the blanket. She releases a tiny moan.

"I'm fine," Caderyn whispers. "Just a bit nauseated." He wipes sweat from his brow.

"I'll bring you some ginger ale and a cool towel."

Once she heads to the back of the airliner, Caderyn closes his eyes again and lingers in early memories with Granger and other members of his clan that have long since passed. He blinks back tears before they have a chance to leave a trail on his cheeks.

The flight attendant reappears and places a bottle of water and ginger ale down on his tray next to a small pack of butter cookies. She hands him the damp towel and stands back for a moment.

"Is there anything else I can get you?" she whispers.

"I'm fine. Thank you. How much longer until we land?"

"About three hours. Let me know if you need anything else."

The steady hum of the jet's engine relaxes Caderyn. He sighs and realizes his life is coming to a bittersweet end. The irony of the transfer stings. He will meet Logan, transfer his memories and magic, and then be killed by the only person who can save his lineage. It's the only way he will live on, the only way his ancestors will continue to exist.

It's the only way Logan and Jasmyn will survive.

~ ~ ~

"How soon will this jet get us to New York?" Patricia asks the pilot sitting at the controls, checking meters and writing in a flight book.

The pilot doesn't look up as he mutters, "Approximately three and a half hours."

"Can you get there faster?"

He looks up Patricia and releases an exasperated sigh. "It's about twenty-four hundred miles to JFK, and the G650 goes 700 miles per hour. We're already traveling faster than any commercial jetliner. If we go any faster, with this much fuel, we risk reaching our destination. If you wish we can land in

Pittsburgh—"

"No, that's fine."

He turns back to his controls and his flight book without another word.

Patricia leaves the cockpit and walks past the single flight attendant to the open door. "Where the hell are they?"

She sees a jeep in the distance approaching the small aircraft. She sighs the instant she recognizes Gustavo driving, but then her stomach tightens when she realizes he's alone— Regina stayed with Brian and Walter at the hospital.

He stops the car, jumps out, and runs up the ramp. He sits down on a rich beige-leather couch built into one side of the cabin and stretching the length of the entire plane.

"How are they?" Patricia asks in a whisper.

Gustavo glances over at Jasmyn sitting at one of four individual seats set around a square coffee table at the other side of the aircraft's cabin. "Walter is conscious. Broken shoulders and dislocated discs—in a lot of pain but he'll be fine. Brian is…"

Jasmyn stares eagerly, but Gustavo can only offer an apologetic frown.

"Brian has brain hemorrhaging. Regina's doing what she can. The doctors too, but…"

When Gustavo moves to sit next to Jasmyn, she waves him away. He steps back and finds another individual seat further back in the plane.

The pilot walks into the cabin from the front of the plane and addresses Patricia. "I'm ready whenever you are ma'am."

"We're still waiting for two more."

As if on cue, Arsen and Logan run up the ramp and pile into the cabin. They throw themselves onto the luxurious leather couch, gasping for breath. Small plumes of dirt and dust tumble off their bodies; loose particles land on the ground around them. The dark gray film all over Arsen's and Logan's bodies give them the appearance of mine workers that narrowly escaped a collapsing cave.

With his face in a tight grimace, Logan leans forward and lowers his head into his hands. Arsen puts his hand on Logan's shoulder and squeezes his muscle. Two deep breaths later, Logan slaps Arsen's hand off his shoulder, stands, and heads to the back of the plane. He finds a bathroom and slams the door shut.

The flight attendant closes the hatch and instructs them to prepare for departure.

"What happened?" Patricia asks Arsen.

After a long sigh, Arsen leans back into the rich leather seat and rubs his face with his hands. He surrenders his arms to the side and stares up at the ceiling. "Logan did what he had to do."

He glances at Jasmyn, and she returns a solemn nod and moves her gaze to the floor in front of her. A mix of sorrow and appreciation crosses Patricia's face, and, without another word, she sits down in a seat at the front and buckles herself in.

~ ~ ~

Kean trembles the instant he feels Granger's passing. Once the torturous ache in his muscles dissipates, he releases a harrowing scream and slams his fist on the tray table in front of him. The tray cracks off its hinges and tumbles to the floor of the plane.

"Am I to depend on no one?"

The co-pilot walks to Kean's seat with a flight attendant following behind him. He straightens his shoulders. "Sir, you'll have to control yourself."

"I apologize." He waves his hand as if batting at an annoying fly.

"If you do not control yourself, I will be forced to report you to the air marshal. You'll be arrested as soon as—"

Kean nods with his eyes closed as his strength returns. The pilot is still speaking when Kean locks eyes with him and quickly mutters a spell. The pilot falls silent.

"How long before we arrive?" Kean's voice is smooth and confident.

"Three hours and forty minutes," the pilot replies monotonously, still staring at Kean.

"You will fly this plane at top speed and get to New York within three hours. You will notify the airport of a pregnant woman about to give birth, a man having a heart attack, or whatever circumstance will give you emergency landing clearance. You will say whatever you have to say to land within three hours. And, you will not bother me again."

The flight attendant stares at Kean in disbelief.

Kean switches his gaze to the flight attendant. "Is that understood?"

Once the trance sinks in, the flight attendant nods. The pilot retreats to the cockpit with the flight attendant following in the same robotic manner.

I can depend on no one.

19

LUCIDITY

"Any news on Brian?" Arsen whispers to Patricia as she sits next to him tapping on her phone. He glances behind his seat to ensure Logan and Jasmyn are still asleep, and spots Gustavo sprawled out on a reclining couch at the back of the plane.

"Regina is doing what she can with her healing powers, but it doesn't look good for Brian. Death is beyond our control."

"Not entirely."

She rolls her eyes in his direction. "Dark magic is not an option... yet. I have committed too many sins to use it carelessly."

"Saving a life is not a careless use of dark magic."

"You're not saving a life—you're preventing a death. Life and death are equally strong entities, and defying either of them has great consequences. And if the conjurer has lived an impure life riddled with deception and treachery, then there is no defense against the darkness."

Arsen rolls his eyes. "You don't have to lecture me. I know the risks."

"As do I."

"Then you know your past sins don't matter as much as your intentions."

"That's a theory. No one knows exactly why some resist its temptation and others are consumed by it. Intentions may play a role, but so do the sorcerer's inner strength, current state of mind, emotional fortitude—"

144

"Yes, there are many internal factors."

"One's aura is weakened by self-loathing and guilt, by the loss of someone you love, from failing to save someone you love." Her throat gets tight as she recalls the penetrating fear of dark magic's hold when she contemplated using it to save Katarina's life, and the utter regret that followed when she decided against it. "Maybe that loss weakens you and makes you susceptible to the darkness's hold."

"Sometimes the death of a loved one, that crushing agony, all that suffering, can make one's aura stronger—like a steel sword forged from burning and hammering iron."

"Forging a sword takes time. Healing from pain like that takes time."

"Some swordsmiths are faster than others."

When Patricia glances his way, Arsen stares at her lips for a moment and then looks away. He clears his throat. "Jasmyn has a long history of treating her sister poorly, has she not?"

Patricia nods.

"And look at how she reacted when her sister died. She executed the entrapment spell and successfully fought off the temptations of dark magic. Her intention, at the time, was pure. How was her aura when she executed the spell?"

"Powerful. A solid blue. I don't think my aura has ever been that strong."

He scans her up and down. "You have a blue aura right now."

"Stronger than mine. And besides, it doesn't mean I can ward off dark magic. There is no guarantee."

"But it means you have a good chance at it."

Patricia sighs and looks away again.

A sad smile tugs at his lips as he recalls how he and Patricia used to discuss the moral obligations of their families, the political climate of their clans, and the limits of their magic until all hours of the night. The memories feel far away, but at the same time, it warms his heart to know he can still have these sorts of discussions with her. At that moment, Arsen feels he's crossed a tricky mountain slope that seemed unconquerable earlier in the day. They are talking, discussing theories together.

"All I know is," Patricia continues, "I would test the darkness only if it meant saving Jasmyn's life. But, not for Brian or anyone else." She looks at Arsen. "I would risk my own life for Jasmyn. Only she matters to me now."

"What about Logan?"

Patricia leans her head back against her seat and closes her eyes. With her eyebrows in a tight furrow, she shakes her head in response to Arsen's question.

"And Gustavo."

After a long breath, and after Patricia forces Gustavo's handsome smile out of her head, she replies, barely above a whisper, "Only Jasmyn."

~ ~ ~

Turbulence wakes Jasmyn from her most recent nightmare where Katarina plummeted to her death down a black chasm in the middle of a desert mountain. She reached for Katarina's hand, but it was just out of reach. The abyss swallowed up her baby sister before she could wake up.

In an earlier nightmare, Katarina fell into a lake where the gravel floor transformed into a whirlpool and pulled her under. The concrete edge of the pond moved backward, foiling Jasmyn's every attempt to grab Katarina's flailing hands before she was pulled underwater.

Jasmyn slams the back of the seat in front of her. *I am*

not the reason Kat is gone. I am NOT the reason Kat is gone.

With her lips pursed, she rises from her seat and heads to the restroom to freshen up. She repeats her mantra while splashing cold water on her face. Tiny droplets drip down her nose and chin as she stands tall and looks in the mirror, recalling the similarities among her dreams. They all start with Katarina holding a book open, with a pen in hand, sitting on a rock or beach at the edge of a lake, pond, or cliff. The wind blows her wispy hair away from her face as she looks at her book and then back up at the sky, oblivious of Jasmyn's presence.

Every time Jasmyn gets closer to Katarina, the serene moment dissolves into a tumultuous scene. A sinkhole swallows up the lake; a tidal wave attacks the beach; an earthquake shakes the mountainside. And, eventually, Katarina dies, her hands just out of Jasmyn's reach and her mouth agape as if she is trying to shout, but no words come out. Not a single sound.

Jasmyn stares at her reflection in the bathroom mirror. *What are you trying to say to me, Kat? Why make me feel your death over and over? The earthquakes and storms and... almost saving you but not saving you... It's as if you want me to suffer. Is that it? Do you want me to suffer? Are you punishing me? Do you blame me for your death? For everything?*

Jasmyn's body trembles, a burning shock passing through her body as if fighting off an icy breeze with internal warmth. She closes her eyes for two seconds before opening them up once more, staring straight into the eyes of the scowling face in the mirror.

Stop it. Stop punishing yourself, damn it!

Another shock traverses her muscles, causing them to vibrate, to flex and relax as heat penetrates the fibers.

It's not my fault.

She holds her breath and presses her lips tighter, glaring

147

at her eyes in the mirror.

It's... not... my... fault!

Cracks burst across the mirror from the center outward. Jasmyn steps back and away, studying the fissures in the glass that span the length of the tiny bathroom. After a moment, she closes her mouth and breathes normally. She finds her broken reflection in the mirror.

I am not the reason Kat is gone. None of this is my fault. No more self-pity.

After wiping her face dry, she marches back to her seat. She exhales forcefully and closes her eyes.

The next time I see you, you will speak to me, Kat, and you will not die.

~ ~ ~

"Took you long enough."

The melodious sound of Katarina's voice pulls Jasmyn's attention away from the sunset on the ocean's horizon. She turns to face her little sister, who is sitting on the white sandy beach with her legs in a crisscross under her lacy, shimmery dress. The wind blows her auburn bangs away from her face and allows Katarina's bucktooth smile to shine.

Jasmyn looks back at the waves crashing far away, narrowing her eyes as she studies the shoreline, the sky, and the distant clouds, commanding everything to stay as it is—calm and under her control. She turns back to face her little sister.

"I've been waiting for you forever!" Katarina says.

Jasmyn laughs at Katarina's exaggerated expression. "You were always so impatient."

With quick motions, Katarina stuffs her pencil into the crook of her journal and closes it. She stands, her dress swaying with her bouncy movements, and throws her arms around her big sister's waist.

As the wind blows against their bodies, Jasmyn can't help but feel the deep bond of sisterhood pass between them—the bond of being real blood sisters as well as sister witches in the same coven. Is this feeling an invention in Jasmyn's mind? A concoction of how she hopes Katarina would feel if she were still alive? A healing mechanism for the loss of the person she cared for most in the entire world, though she never showed it? Was Katarina forgiving her for all those years of torment? Was Jasmyn forgiving herself?

Perhaps. In any case, Jasmyn waves off the equal probabilities of these truths and hugs her baby sister with all her might.

"I'm not impatient. I'm eight," Katarina whispers.

"You're eight going on forty-five."

Katarina nods. "It's true. I've always been mature for my age."

Jasmyn takes Katarina's hand, and they stroll along the shoreline. "Too mature. Sometimes annoyingly mature."

"Is that why you hated me so much?"

Thunder roars from behind, and they stop walking. Jasmyn glares back miles away to where the storm is forming and rolls her eyes at the dark gray clouds gathering. *Even if you bring on a typhoon, you're not tricking me. This is my dream. Kat is my sister. I'm in control here.*

The thunder stops, and the clouds disperse, giving way to the evening sky painted in a deep orange hue. Black silhouettes of seagulls glide over the ocean in an elegant dance as Jasmyn pulls Katarina along to continue their walk.

"I never hated you."

Katarina nods. "I know."

They walk in silence as Jasmyn collects her thoughts.

"I was angry at everyone. I was jealous of the attention everyone gave you. I was awful."

"But Nana said that Mom and Dad should have—"

"I know what Nana said. Mom and Dad share some of the blame, but I need to own some as well. You were sick, and I was selfish. I guess I wasn't smart enough to see things as clearly as you. If only I were a mature kid like you."

A hint of a smile crosses Katarina's face.

"As I got older, I let jealousy cloud everything. I should have seen that happening, should have been more forgiving of everyone who I thought did me wrong. Then, maybe, it wouldn't have taken me so long to forgive myself."

"But you're okay now, right? I mean, you understand that what happened to me is not your fault."

"Yeah. But, it took me this long to actually believe it. I'm sorry I treated you so poorly. I was a horrible sister. Can you ever forgive me?"

"Of course."

Like most eight-year-old children who jump from topic to topic at lightning speed, Katarina shouts, "Look what I have!" She raises her book to Jasmyn's face to show her what's written on the cover. "It's my journal! I have loads of stories in here— mostly stories about us, real ones and pretend ones too. And some stories Nana told me, new ones that were never in the *Book of Whispers*. Look!" She flips through the pages to show Jasmyn the abundance of hand-written pages. "It's completely full!"

"You wrote all this?"

"Yes and no. I copied a lot from Nana's journals."

"You've read Nana's journals?"

"Of course! Haven't you read them yet?"

Jasmyn inhales a rush of air as she awakens in her seat

aboard the plane to New York. She pulls herself up to her feet and stumbles to the last row where two cardboard boxes hold all of Agatha's relics. At the bottom of the second box, she finds three leather-bound journals filled with cursive handwriting she immediately recognizes as her grandmother's. She traces the intricate carvings on the leather cover of the topmost book with her index finger, bends back the spine, and turns to the first page.

20

AGATHA'S JOURNALS

The flickering lights in the jet's cabin grab Jasmyn's attention away from the last few pages of Agatha's final journal. The flight attendant appears at the front of the plane and announces the jet will be landing at JFK in approximately thirty minutes. Jasmyn resumes reading the entry.

~ ~ ~

April 14th 1950

There is nothing for me now. No lineage, cousins, extended relatives to care for. I have two coven sisters still alive, yet we haven't spoken in an eternity. I am a sister without my sisters, estranged from my coven, from the only women who understand me. But they will never truly understand. They will never know everything there is to know. Regina is too young, and Patricia is too careless and carefree. I need to figure this out on my own—this is my task, my sentence.

It's been decades since the destruction, and I had hoped something would appear by now to guide my course of action, give me direction. A universal sign? Yet, nature has gone silent. The winds say nothing to me. I'm abandoned by all that I know in my world.

Why am I still here? Why did I survive? Why outlive my family, my coven, my people? I have lost my way.

I had hoped that, one day, after all my suffering, I would find some sort of happiness. But, I haven't. I have nothing to live for. I can't go on this way. There is only one thing left to do.

I swore to Mother that I would never use this magic unless my life depended on it. Until now, I have fulfilled my vow. I'm sorry, Mother, but I must break my promise. I have to find the Isle of Enid and use the time-reversal spell. I will try to get a handle on the dragons before they get out of control, before they destroy our coven. My intentions are good, and so the darkness should not have a hold on me. I know I will not fail.

~ ~ ~

After a long sigh, Jasmyn closes the journal and sets it down on her lap. She shuts her eyes and imagines her grandmother, at a younger age, walking along one of the California beaches she mentions in her journal entries. The mid-May sun sits high over the ocean's crystal-blue sky, kissing her face with a hint of the approaching summer. Her flowery dress whips against the ocean's breeze as she walks barefoot across the sand, lost in thought of all things past and present. Jasmyn can almost feel the sea wind caressing her cheeks.

A smile crosses her face as she recalls her grandmother's story of how she met her grandfather on a beach in California. Elliot's young golden retriever broke from his leash and ran along the shore for several minutes—untamed, wild, and free—before it found Agatha and leaped into her arms, knocking her down to the ground. The pup licked her face profusely until Elliot arrived and begged Agatha for forgiveness. When their eyes met, they fell in love instantly.

"What are you thinking of that has you smiling like that?" Patricia asks as she sits down in the seat next to Jasmyn.

"About the first time Nana met Grandpa."

"Ah, yes. The famous dog attack."

"It was a puppy." Jasmyn smiles. "And it didn't attack her; it jumped into her arms."

"Right. A one-year-old, seventy-pound, golden retriever puppy attack. Those dogs are big."

"Still, the way they met, it's kind of romantic. Did you know Grandpa Elliot back then?"

Patricia sits back in her seat and stares down at her hands folded on her lap. "I met him several times, but I didn't get to know him well. Back then, I was… different."

"Different how?"

"I was going through…" Patricia sighs, "an anarchy phase."

Jasmyn raises an eyebrow. "Anarchy phase?"

"Yeah. I didn't want to hide who we were. I did magic openly without caring if anyone saw. California was going through a progressive era, accepting everyone of all races and religions. It was perfect for us, at least I thought so. Agatha was more conservative, more reserved. We argued a lot back then about the direction of our coven. I was so full of myself. I was such a jerk."

A few seconds pass in silence before Patricia continues. "Finna went back in time, sacrificed her entire family, to save us all. Finna's pain became Agatha's pain. She had to deal with all of that, and there I was acting like a selfish ass." She shakes her head. "What Agatha must have thought of me."

"I don't think Nana would have called you selfish."

"She did, once, and she was right." Patricia sighs. "If I had known what your grandmother went through, I *know* I would've behaved differently."

Jasmyn stares down at her own hands. *That makes two of*

us.

The flight attendant returns and orders Patricia and Jasmyn to buckle themselves in as the pilot starts his descent. The airplane shakes violently as Jasmyn secures her seat belt, and she drops Agatha's journal.

Patricia bends over and picks it up. She stares at the cover and sighs. "Did you find anything interesting?"

"Oh, tons. I read all three." Jasmyn gestures to the side to show Patricia the two other books on the seat next to her.

Patricia lowers her gaze. "Did she write about me?"

"Not in the way you think. She didn't say anything bad about you. She was just... sad. And maybe lonely. She missed you."

Dryness forms in Patricia's throat. She closes her eyes and forces a swallow.

"You should read Nana's last entry."

Patricia opens the journal to the page with the satin strand, her hands trembling. As her eyes pass along the words of the last entry, her mouth drops open. Once she finishes, she lifts her eyes and stares forward for a few seconds as the revelation unfolds. "That's why she was so desperate to find the Isle of Enid. She can execute the time-reversal spell only there."

"Find it? Was it lost?"

"It vanished."

A perplexed look appears on Jasmyn's face.

"Back then, we didn't keep coordinates or sailing maps or such things. We'd sail from Europe, and our magic ties to the island would pull us in, like a magnetic force tugging on our muscles. Our magic directed us home. Then, in April of 1905 or 1906—I can't recall exactly—Agatha got weary of Norway, where we lived at the time, and we set sail for home. But we couldn't find it. The pull was gone. We sailed from several northern ports, but we never felt the pull."

"You said she was desperate?"

Patricia nods. "I, personally, didn't care much about going home. There was so much painful history there. But Agatha tried to sail back multiple times and failed. She would go through bouts of depression. She tried and tried again, hiring sailors from different ports. I never understood why she was so desperate to go home."

Patricia glances at the journal page, scowls, and then slams the book shut. "Didn't she learn anything from Finna? What was she thinking?"

"Maybe she felt that there was nothing for her to lose. It's not like she had a family like Finna had when she made the decision."

Regina and I weren't in her life, not really. Patricia huffs. *She had no one to lose.*

"Did she ever try to… kill herself?"

"Our coven's magic doesn't allow it."

"So, she was trapped."

Patricia nods, leans her head back on the seat, and closes her eyes tight as she realizes that she was absent during Agatha's weakest moment. *Thank goodness you weren't allowed to kill yourself. I don't know whether I could have survived that.*

As she recalls all their disagreements, all the times Patricia stormed away from Agatha leaving her sister crying from the intensity of their arguments, a pressure forms in her chest. *Maybe it was best that you didn't tell me. At that time, as crazy as I was, as much drugs and partying as I was doing, I probably would have caused even more harm if I'd known the truth. I would have accused you of betraying me and our coven.*

She turns away from Jasmyn and blinks back tears. *I was such a horrible person back then. I'm so sorry, Agatha. I should have been there for you.*

After regaining her composure, Patricia opens the journal to the page of that last entry and notices the date. She clears her throat. "This entry was written just before she met Elliot, maybe a day or two before the dog attack."

"So, she met Grandpa, and it was love at first sight." Jasmyn smiles.

Patricia nods and releases a long sigh. "And after what Finna went through, and what came after, there was no way Agatha would sacrifice her chance at happiness."

21

NEGOTIATIONS

"Mister, you're going to miss the landing."

The little girl's sweet voice draws Caderyn's eyes open, awakening him from an unexpected, deep sleep. He blinks several times before focusing his vision on the little girl's pink shirt with its cheery blue bird on the front.

"See." She points out the window, then gasps when the plane touches the ground. "Landing is always the scariest part." Her squinting eyes and wide smile produce tiny dimples on her cheeks. She looks back out the window, her auburn locks spilling over her shoulders.

"You're a brave girl to fly all alone."

She shrugs. "My parents are divorced. I fly back and forth a lot. I'm used to it."

As the plane comes to a complete stop at a JFK terminal, Caderyn identifies the signature aura of a supernatural being. It's Kean, and he is in the air. His aircraft is about to land.

He waits for the other passengers to depart the aircraft before standing and reaching for his small leather carry-on bag in the overhead compartment. He looks down at the little girl sitting quietly in her seat with her hands folded. "Aren't you getting off?" Caderyn asks as he pulls down his bag.

"I have to wait for the flight attendant. She's going to take me to my mom."

Caderyn senses Kean's presence growing, along with the presence of another clansman on the ground. Although Caderyn can't hide his aura's signature from his brothers, he can expedite the off-boarding process and steer everyone away from Kean. After whispering several words under his breath, a flight attendant comes to fetch Sasha, and the other flight attendant and the two pilots file out of the plane.

Sasha slides out of their row and straightens her pink shirt. She looks up at Caderyn and tilts her head, furrowing her eyebrows as if she's studying Caderyn's face. "It could be worse. I could be flying to California, which is six hours more than New York. Or nine. I always get the hours mixed up." She shrugs her shoulders. "It all depends on how you look at things. My mom always tells me that no matter how bad things are, it can always be worse."

Caderyn smiles. "That's very insightful. Your mother is a smart woman."

"My mom is awesome!" Sasha shouts and turns to face the flight attendant, her wavy locks bouncing behind her. With a nod and a genuine smile, Caderyn thanks the flight attendant for taking care of Sasha and places a protection spell on them. Before she turns to step through the aircraft's door, Sasha looks back and waves vigorously at Caderyn. "Bye, mister!"

The little girl reminds him of his own daughter's spunk and positivity. So much has transpired since those happier days that he's forgotten what it's like to interact with an innocent child. The last few minutes talking with Sasha has infused Caderyn with a feeling of renewal—a stark contrast to the hopelessness he's been feeling for a long while.

His back straightens as he remembers that Kean can end it all for Sasha without thinking twice. Although Sasha isn't his daughter, she is someone's Agatha.

Within seconds, Caderyn strides from the off-boarding ramp and into the terminal building. He spreads his hands and speaks in a stern tone—the spell clears the surrounding area. A slow-moving mob forms as people walk in the same direction without speaking. Officers, passengers, flight attendants, pilots and other airport personnel all move at a robotic daze, their monotonous footsteps echoing in the wide corridors. They head toward the entrance of the terminal and exit onto the roads and out toward the parking lots.

Once he's satisfied the terminal building is clear of any potential casualties, Caderyn pushes through the maintenance doors and walks out onto the tarmac. He crosses the taxiway and redirects a tow truck attached to an aircraft to the far end of the airport. He heads toward the central tower and wills the people who manage the controls to halt all air traffic into and out of the airport. He turns around to face the terminal building, where he continues to track Kean's aura.

There is no need to harm anyone, Kean. If you wish to fight me, come and meet me out in the open. I'm ready for you.

~ ~ ~

The crisp winds blow along Kean's jawline as he walks out of the terminal and out onto the airport runways. With a savage grin, he pictures the caress as a sign that the universe is aligned with his goals. His time has finally come.

Abandoned vehicles and airplane loading equipment are scattered along his path. The silence around him brings a disgusted smirk to his face.

You save these mortals who would kill you the instant they learned what you are.

From the south side of the bay bordering the airport, a brotherly aura captures Kean's attention. Within seconds, a scruffy, bearded, seven-foot man materializes a few feet in front of Kean wearing a brown, blue, and black flannel shirt, worn-out jeans, and mountain boots.

"You came after all, Breccan."

He nods in salutation. "It's my duty to our clan."

"Then you are in agreement with my plans?" After scanning his body for weaponry, Kean faces Breccan squarely. "Or, are you here to help Caderyn?"

Breccan glances around the empty airport. "If I were here for Caderyn, you would be dead by now. I have all the right reasons to kill you."

"State your intentions plainly, brother. We've been through too much together; we're beyond trying to deceive one another."

Breccan scowls as the howl of the wind cuts the silence between them. He gazes out across the airport once more, his eyes following the string of lights along the distant runway borders. He inhales the cold midnight air and turns back to face Kean.

"I've had forty-two children, twenty-six males. I've recognized them as my heirs, but nothing has come of it. None of my children have been able to procreate, not a single one. I've watched my bloodline begin and end, over and over again. I've continued to have more children in the hope that our clan's magic would allow me an heir and free me from this misery. I can't die by mortal means. I can't kill myself. And those whom I've asked to kill me have more than ample reason to keep me alive rather than ease my suffering."

"I won't kill you, Breccan."

"Of course not. You need me; like you needed all of us to battle dragons that you knew were unstoppable."

Kean sighs and rolls his eyes. "No one knew the extent of their powers."

"The elders did. They warned you, and Caderyn. Yet, you ignored them, kept that bit of information secret from the rest of us, and sent our clansmen into battle. My home was on the outskirts of our island, the first home to be burnt to the ground; my family didn't have a chance. My powers had no effect on those dragons. You knew they were indestructible, and you didn't warn us."

"The elders only suspected it. There was no guarantee." Kean frowns. "It was not my decision to—"

"No, it wasn't. It was Caderyn's. But you were part of his council. You advised him."

"Yes." Kean meets Breccan's glare with his eyebrows furrowed in anger. "And if you were in my shoes, you would have advised your clan leader in the same manner, to defend your clansmen and families at any cost. At all costs. We made decisions with the information we believed to be true, and I will not apologize for that."

"Even now you can't take some semblance of responsibility." Breccan huffs.

"Finna and her coven killed your family, not me. She released the dragons upon us. She betrayed Caderyn and the clan. She rode the black dragon that set the entire coastline on fire, and she gave them the order to slay everyone on our island."

"I need no reminding."

"Then help me destroy the coven."

"To what end?" Breccan shouts. "You want to kill Caderyn and end the coven to gain power for yourself. That's of no interest to me. You can take your lofty goals and—"

"The elder has shared the time-reversal spell with me."

Breccan cocks his head and narrows his eyes at Kean. "Finna's time-reversal spell?"

Kean nods.

A throaty guffaw escapes Breccan's mouth. "You said yourself that the elder's visions are not guaranteed to be accurate."

"Ryland has sworn to me that it will work."

Waving his hand, Breccan turns and walks away.

"Even if the time-reversal spell doesn't work," Kean shouts, "you will have taken revenge on Finna's coven by killing her lineage. Jasmyn is Finna's kin and the heir to her magic."

A stir in Breccan's chest brings him to a halt. He turns back around to face Kean, lifting his chin and narrowing his eyes. "Go on."

"Ryland tells me that Jasmyn's blood will enable us to release the last Gregorn Dragon from its prison—release it under our control. So, in case the time-reversal spell doesn't work, we have other options."

Breccan steps toward Kean, eying him skeptically. "And if the time-reversal spell works?"

Kean smiles. "If it works, then we'll go back in time and wipe out Finna's coven before she has an inkling of our intentions. And, you can be with your family, Kora, Fenly—"

Breccan steps away from Kean, throwing up a hand to make him stop talking. He straightens his grimace as visions of his four young daughters engulfed in flames flash through his mind, memories that inflict fresh wounds with each recollection, wounds that time can't seem to heal. His heart aches as he recalls wallowing next to the piles of ashes left behind, the smallest of the black mounds representing his two-year-old daughter Jan. Even centuries later, he still feels the black, grainy texture that scorched his hands when he pored over his family's remains, cursing the universe as he pressed his hands through the middle of the black powder in utter disbelief.

The torture of these lucid memories stirs up an

uncontrollable desire for revenge. He failed at protecting his loved ones. He failed at taking revenge against Finna's coven. He has failed repeatedly at killing himself.

He will fail no longer.

"I'll help you, Kean, but you must promise me one thing."

"Anything."

"I want to kill Finna's kin, the girl Jasmyn. I want her to know who I am, to know what Finna did to me and my family, and to see that it is *me* who kills her."

Kean nods. "Her death is yours."

They both grab each other's right forearm and pull in for a clansman's embrace.

After he releases Kean's arm, Breccan gazes out toward the direction of Caderyn's weakening aura. "Only two things can come out of this endeavor. One, we succeed and avenge ourselves on Finna and her coven, and I get to see my family again. Or two, you fail, and Finna's coven kills us both." He huffs, a smirk breaking his grimace. "I prefer revenge. I want the look of terror in her eyes. I deserve it." He spits to the side and wipes his mouth. "But death would also suffice."

22

SACRIFICES

Gustavo spent the last half hour packing Agatha's relics into backpacks for simplified transportation. When the plane finally comes to a complete stop, the pilot calls out to Gustavo. Everyone rises from their seats and stretches.

The pilot turns to Gustavo when he enters the cockpit. "Something's going on. They've halted all airport traffic."

"Did they give a reason?"

"No. But, this is JFK. They never close. It must be something big."

In the main cabin, Arsen looks out the window as Gustavo hands Logan and Jasmyn their backpacks. Patricia leans in next to Arsen and follows his gaze.

Arsen grunts. "They're here, Kean and Caderyn. And Breccan is with them."

"Breccan?" Gustavo asks.

"He's a clansman."

"Another one?" Gustavo rolls his eyes and huffs. "How many more are there?"

"He's the last one." Arsen says. "I promise."

The cabin doors open, and Gustavo runs down the steps to a military truck that's awaiting their arrival. He directs everyone to pile in before he climbs into the front seat of the passenger side. Arsen directs the driver toward Caderyn's aura.

"What happens to Logan if Kean and Breccan kill Caderyn?" Patricia asks, glancing at Arsen.

"If they kill Caderyn before the transfer is complete, Logan will have some of Caderyn's power, but he won't know how to use it, just as Jasmyn doesn't know how to use Agatha's. Logan won't have all of Caderyn's knowledge or memories."

"But how much of Caderyn's magic will he have?"

Arsen shrugs. "It's hard to predict. Magic transfers as it wishes."

"What do you mean, 'as it wishes'?"

Arsen shares a glance with Patricia and Jasmyn. "Your coven's custom is to transfer magic through touch between the sorceress and the heir she chooses." He locks his gaze with Jasmyn. "Your grandmother chose no one, nor did she touch you before she died, and yet, here you are with her magic. The normal or customary means of the transfer of magic was rejected, but your family's magic chose to live on by other means."

He looks at Logan. "Our clan differs in that the heir is chosen for us by our clan's magic. It chooses an heir from one of the sorcerer's kin. But, that's not a given. Breccan has tried many times to select an heir. He's had many male children, whom he's recognized as his kin, yet none of them were chosen by the magic. The only thing that is certain is that once the transfer is initiated, for our clan, it's completed upon death. The sorcerer is killed by the successor, or both are killed by someone else."

Jasmyn scowls.

Arsen raises his eyebrows. "Magic transfers as it wishes. We don't control it; just like we don't control nature or the universe. It exists however it chooses, and we abide."

Jasmyn shakes her head and folds her arms tightly across her chest. "I hate this."

Arsen huffs. "Which part?"

"The not-having-control-over-anything part. I didn't choose to be Nana's successor, and Logan didn't choose to be Caderyn's heir." She glances at Logan sitting behind her. "Neither of us want it; yet, we were 'chosen' to carry on our family's freaking magic."

"Maybe that's why you were both chosen."

She glares at Arsen and then rolls her eyes away from him. "Magic can kiss my ass."

"That's very eloquent, Jasmyn."

"Jaz is right," Logan says. "For once, I completely agree with my sister. Magic has been nothing but trouble. Magic can go kiss my ass, too."

Jasmyn glances over her shoulder at Logan and nods, and he nods back. It's a relief and a satisfaction to declare their opinion for everyone to hear, including Magic.

~ ~ ~

After a couple of minutes driving along an airport road, an explosion from far away shakes the vehicle. The driver swerves but soon regains control of the truck. "Is everyone okay?" he shouts.

Gustavo looks back and then returns his gaze to the road ahead. "Just keep going."

The driver nods and then squints his eyes at something in the air. "What is that?"

Arsen leans toward the front of the car and sees a large piece of flaming metal heading their way. Although the driver speeds up, he can't escape the airplane wing's trajectory. Arsen places a shield at the last second, but the impact knocks the car onto its left side. The metal squeals against the concrete floor as it slides down the road.

The loud screech ends with a crash as the truck slams into an electric pole, the wires snapping and flapping wildly around them.

Patricia crawls up and out through the rear side door with Arsen right behind her. Logan climbs up and reaches back down to help Jasmyn up and out.

Arsen steps away from the truck to read his brothers' auras. "Kean and Breccan, they're fighting Caderyn. He's still alive, but hurt. He can't hold them off much longer."

"Patricia!" Jasmyn shouts as Logan tries to dislodge Gustavo from the front passenger seat.

Arsen runs to the front of the truck. The bumper is smashed inward, and several metal street signs are jutting into the hood and windshield. "Everyone, stand clear." He raises his arms and recites a spell, slowly lifting the vehicle and placing it carefully on the ground on its four wheels. Patricia runs to the passenger side, and Arsen checks on the driver. The lifeless young soldier's face is covered in blood and shards of glass.

Arsen shakes his head, and then glances over at Gustavo in the passenger seat. A thick piece of metal pierces Gustavo's side.

Patricia raises her eyes to meet Arsen's gaze, with her mouth agape, her eyes failing to hide her worry. She recites a healing prayer, passing her hands over his torso in a circular motion. Over and over she repeats the spell, pressing her eyes closed tighter. She lowers her hands to her side and glances up at Arsen, her eyes red with unshed tears. "If you take it out, he'll bleed to death," she whispers, losing her voice as she stifles a cry.

As Patricia continues her healing spells, Arsen notices a change in her normally guarded aura. Her shield is down, and he sees her thoughts and memories clearly, as if they were his own.

He watches as Patricia recalls her sisters dying in her arms from battle wounds she could not heal. Her sisters gaze upon her with pleading eyes, their last hope. But, Patricia is unable to fulfill their dying request. She relives dozens of deaths that could have been prevented by Regina or another sorceress with stronger healing powers, but these women were fated to die in Patricia's arms.

The image of a battered Katarina lying on the ground appears in Patricia's mind, and Patricia shuts her eyes tight, but tears trickle out anyway. Arsen listens to Patricia's lament. *How many more deaths must I suffer? How many more people must die because of me?*

Then, Gustavo's heartbeat stops. Patricia gasps.

Arsen runs around the truck to the passenger side. "Move!"

He pulls Patricia away from Gustavo and squeezes into the front section of the truck. He places his closed fist against Gustavo's chest and closes his eyes in concentration as he recites a spell. With his other hand hovering over the wound, Arsen drags the piece of metal out of Gustavo's midsection. Blood oozes out as the metal is removed. With his eyes still closed, Arsen continues his focus on Gustavo's wounds.

Gustavo opens his eyes and wails, cursing aloud as the spell burns his insides and heals the torn flesh and organs. After five seconds of screaming, the shock of the surgery renders him unconscious.

As the spell completes, a force presses upon Arsen's aura, stiffening and squeezing his muscles, and at the same time pulling the muscle fibers apart. Heat burns at his skin and traverses his entire body. His breathing grows heavy as the darkness intensifies, pulling him inward and outward, clouding his mind. It tempts him with promises of power, of strength and glory, of fulfilling his every selfish desire.

He shuts his eyes and clenches his fists to fight it off, and thinks of Patricia, of the caramel glimmer in her honest eyes, of her warm smile, of the tears rolling down her cheeks, of her suffering.

Then, with a gasp, he's released from the paralyzing hold. His shoulders fall forward and he takes a minute to catch his breath. When he opens his eyes he finds Patricia scowling at him with her fingertips aimed at his body.

"Are you insane?" Patricia shouts. "Logan needs you to defeat Kean and help Caderyn complete the transfer, and you sacrifice yourself for Gustavo? If you had been taken by the darkness, I would've had to kill you!" She lowers her arms and shakes her head. "Why would you risk that?"

Arsen sighs. "You were suffering."

"What?"

"I saw how much you suffered in your coven, losing your sisters, having them die in your arms. I didn't want to see you suffer anymore."

With a forceful tug, Patricia pulls Arsen out of the car, picks him up by his shirt, and slams him on the ground. "I guarantee you that even Gustavo would agree with me when I say we are to sacrifice ourselves for Jasmyn or Logan only, and no one else. Do you understand?"

As he looks into her angry eyes, Arsen is satisfied with his decision. *Anger is better than sorrow.*

She tightens her grip on his shirt. "Do you understand!"

"Yes. I understand. It won't happen again."

"Swear to it!"

He lifts a hand to his heart. "I swear, with all the powers I have in me, with every single breath from this second forward, I'll sacrifice myself only for Jasmyn or Logan."

"And don't ever read my thoughts! Ever!"

One last slam against the concrete floor and Patricia releases her grip on Arsen. She moves to Gustavo to check his wounds. Logan helps her carry Gustavo to the back of the truck where they lay him flat on his back and cover him up with a blanket.

Arsen glances up at Jasmyn. "I didn't mean to risk you or Logan."

Jasmyn stares down at him with her arms crossed. "I know. I can feel your intentions."

"Ah. I forgot Finna had that gift." Arsen grunts as he stands up tall and dusts himself off. "Does it hurt—my good intentions, whatever it is that you feel from me?"

"No. Good intentions don't hurt. Bad ones do."

"Yet, you don't trust me. You still think I'm a threat."

She points at him. "Don't you dare read my mind."

"I can't read your mind; you shield it well." He stretches his arms back and twists his side to stretch his back muscles. "But, I don't need to read your mind to know you don't trust me. The way you look at me says it all."

Jasmyn rolls her eyes.

"I saved your uncle's life, does that mean nothing to you?"

"You saved my uncle's life to get on Patricia's good side. You're trying to win her back."

He chuckles. "Who's reading whose mind now?"

"I can't read minds, but your intentions are clear."

"Then you know I only have good intentions for you."

"Whether they're good doesn't matter. They're selfish. You're only here for Patricia."

Arsen chuckles as he glances toward Patricia and Logan who have begun the trek toward Caderyn and Kean's battle at the next terminal. "It's true. I'm here because I love her. I love her so much that I saved the life of the man who will probably win her heart and steal her from me, just so she wouldn't suffer another death in her arms."

He starts walking, and Jasmyn follows next to him.

"I love her so much that I'll do everything in my power to ensure your safety. I'd sacrifice my own life to save yours."

"Me? Why?"

"Because losing you is the worst possible thing that could happen to Patricia. Losing you, Jasmyn, will kill her."

~ 23 ~

RIGHTEOUSNESS

After centuries of leadership over the Foreman Clan, Caderyn finds himself at the mercy of his oldest clan brother and cousin, Kean. With a piece of metal sticking through his right leg and another through his right shoulder, Caderyn body is weakening. Airplane parts burn in a roaring fire behind him, setting an appropriate backdrop for what appears to be the final moments of his life.

He fails to stand when Kean and Breccan arrive in front of him. No matter how he commands them to stop their attack, they don't obey. Sensing Logan nearby, he concentrates his magic on his shield.

Arsen, if you can still hear me, you must hurry.

Breccan spits to the side. "The great Caderyn, on his knees. What would your father say to this?"

Caderyn scowls up at the two smug faces. His shoulders fall forward when he exhales, feeling the force of their auras pounding upon his own weakened aura. He slams a spray of light at Breccan's feet, creating a crack in the concrete, and Breccan steps back and away. A smirk crosses Caderyn's face. "Even now, Breccan, I can still move you."

A swift kick to the head flips Caderyn onto his backside. The pieces of metal piercing his body rub along his muscles, making him roar with pain as he rolls. He uses the little power he has left to numb some of the pain and reinforce his shield. He glares up at his clan brothers.

"What is it that you asked of me several centuries ago, Breccan?" Caderyn coughs up blood and spits it out in front of him. "Ah, yes. You begged me to kill you. To end your life." He manages to get on one knee and look at Breccan with narrowed eyes. "We all know what *your* father, and every one of your clansmen, would say to that."

With an uppercut swing, Breccan sends Caderyn tumbling twelve feet to the right. The tubular metal rod in his thigh rips out, exposing raw flesh, and the other metal rod twists in his shoulder. Even with his limbs ripped and tortured, Caderyn finds the strength to rise to one knee and glare up at his brothers.

"Do you recall the advice you gave me about Breccan? 'He's the weakest of us; we could do without him.'" Caderyn coughs again. "Those were your words, Kean. Do you recall?"

Breccan narrows his eyes at Kean.

"He's lying." Kean says, rolling his eyes. "Don't listen to him."

Caderyn notices Breccan's confusion. "Has Kean told you his plan? To interrupt my transfer ceremony, take over the leadership from the very beginning, and give the Foreman Clan a new alternate history."

Both men stand before Caderyn with their hands in fists. Breccan glances at Kean from the corner of his eye as Caderyn speaks.

"He promises a grander history filled with more wars, more battles, more lands to conquer." Caderyn coughs, and then clears his throat. "You won't have to worry about losing your family, Breccan." Caderyn huffs. "Because, if he succeeds, your family may never exist."

Kean slaps Caderyn with the back of his right hand, and Caderyn falls to the side.

Breccan turns his entire body toward Kean, glaring at

him for an explanation. A few silent seconds pass as Breccan quickly recalls memories of his wife and daughters, his mother and father, and his siblings—memories that could be obliterated if Kean changes even a shred of the past. He raises a finger and points to Kean. "You promised me my family."

Kean adjusts his shirt sleeve. "What does it matter? You won't remember a thing."

When Breccan strikes at Kean, Kean avoids the blow and lifts both his arms to blast Breccan halfway across the terminal runway. He follows up with several plane parts slamming down upon his body, pounding him into the ground, leaving Breccan unconscious.

"He never saw past his own interests." Kean turns back to Caderyn.

"Unlike you, Kean?"

"What I do is for the good of our people. For the greatness of the Foreman Clan."

One more backhanded strike sends Caderyn rolling onto his back, the rod still jutting out of his shoulder. He lies flat on the ground with his arms and legs spread wide, gasping for air. The pain shoots to his temples and bounces around in his head, and he presses his eyes tight to numb it.

When he hears Kean's footsteps getting closer, he closes his eyes and envisions Finna in a white frock holding hands with a young Agatha in a flowery dress. Both walk barefoot across a green meadow scattered with daisies; both smile up at him.

In a swift move, Kean lifts the pipe that had ripped out of Caderyn's leg and drives it straight through Caderyn's torso. He leans in close, drilling the pipe into the concrete as Caderyn's face contorts in agony.

A wicked smile fills Kean's face as he drinks in the fear in Caderyn's eyes. He leans in to hear his last breaths. "He will never be our leader. Your kin, your bloodline, will die with you."

~ ~ ~

Logan drops to his knees behind a mangled truck and wails in agony. He shouts so loud that Arsen muffles his mouth and calls Patricia to help. Arsen pushes Logan down on the ground and holds his body as his arms flail and his legs kick out uncontrollably.

"What's happening?" Patricia asks as Arsen struggles with Logan's seizure.

"I don't know. Something must have happened to Caderyn. We have to get Logan to Caderyn before they kill him."

"We're still about two hundred feet away."

Patricia looks across the airport runway to where Breccan lies unconsciousness under a pile of rubble. Kean stands at the other end of the runway just a few steps from Caderyn.

"You're going to have to carry him." Patricia tells Arsen.

Logan's seizures stop and he lies down on his back, breathing heavy but still conscious. Jasmyn runs to his side and drops to her knees.

"Jasmyn," Patricia says, "can you take over my cloaking spell?"

Jasmyn nods, stands and raises her arms.

"I'll distract Kean."

Patricia runs out into the middle of the runway, lifting up vehicles and metallic rubble and slamming them into the ground. She grabs Kean's attention, and he stands to face her with his hands in fists and a cruel smirk across his face.

A refrigerator-size piece of broken airplane hits Patricia

from behind and sends her tumbling fifty feet forward, her head smacking against the ground as she rolls. She finally stops rolling and lays flat on the ground with her arms splayed out. She rises to her feet and rubs the back of her head and neck, and glances back toward where the missile originated.

Breccan now stands in front of the pile of rubble he was under just moments earlier.

"You were always the gentleman, Breccan."

With a snarl on his face, Breccan points to Kean across the field, past Patricia, and shouts, "I will deal with you, scoundrel, once I have destroyed this witch!" He cracks his knuckles and marches towards Patricia. "You have no idea how long I've waited for this moment."

Breccan rushes forward at top speed with his arms outstretched. Lightning explodes from his hands and hits Patricia's shield. Kean shoots thick bolts of lightning from the opposite direction. Patricia's defense weakens from the assault, and she deflects their power. Cracks form in the concrete below, and she loses her balance and falls to her knees. Patricia wails in agony as their attack slowly penetrates her shield.

Arsen lifts Logan to his feet. "Can you walk?"

With a painful grimace on his face, Logan nods.

He turns to Jasmyn. "Take Logan to Caderyn. He must complete the transfer before Caderyn dies."

Before Jasmyn could respond to Arsen's request, Arsen runs into the field and whips Breccan back several yards, digging his body into the concrete and forming a deep channel in the runway. Airplane parts and rubble fly across the airfield as Kean and Breccan battle Patricia and Arsen. The ground quakes upon every impact, and the night air grows thick with smoke and the scent of burning metal.

As the four sorcerers fight, Jasmyn and Logan make a

run for Caderyn. With Logan limping from the pain throbbing from his stomach out to his limbs, Jasmyn recites a spell that helps propel them forward while still holding up their cloak.

A blast from the battle reverberates across the entire airport, and Jasmyn and Logan tumble to the ground. Jasmyn picks Logan up and pulls his arm around her shoulders. She leans his weight on her body and hobbles toward Caderyn's position as quickly as she can.

Another explosion rumbles the ground and fissures in the concrete appear around them. Jasmyn loses her balance, and Logan falls forward into an enormous crevice six feet deep.

Logan lands hard on his feet, breaking both his legs at the shins. He rolls onto his side and screams at the top of his lungs. Jasmyn tumbles and rolls down into the hole, landing hard against her backpack. Something crashes above them on the ground level, and smoke and dirt splash against their faces.

"Logan!" she shouts, grunting as she pushes herself to her feet.

He coughs hard. "Jasmyn!"

Another explosion above sends a shower of rubble into their hole. Jasmyn raises her arms and produces a thick gust of wind with an elemental spell. As the smoke and dust clears, Jasmyn runs to Logan. When she pulls him up, his broken legs give out, and he falls to the ground like a puppet without strings.

She uses her magic to make him lighter and lifts him out of the crevice. She tosses both backpacks up and climbs out of the hole, grunting aloud as her muscles fight through the bruises. Once on top, she sees Caderyn lying on the floor—he's now only seventy feet away.

Jasmyn's body is battered and drained, and her magic can't lift Logan as easily as before. She puts Logan's arm around her shoulders and lifts him as much as her magic allows. With one heavy step at a time, she drags Logan forward.

More fissures open in the ground beneath Jasmyn's feet. She struggles under Logan's weight and loses balance as another tremor shakes the tarmac. She throws Logan to the side to avoid falling into another hole, and he howls as his body slams against the concrete, just fifteen feet away from Caderyn.

Just as she moves to reach Logan again, Jasmyn catches a glimpse of a ball of fire soaring toward her head. She stands quickly and puts up both hands to block it. The impact against her shield sends her flying.

She hits the ground past Caderyn and rolls for a couple feet. Her head spins, bright lights flash before her eyes, and her back and neck throb with pain. She closes her eyes for a moment and squeezes them tight. Nausea threatens her, but she swallows back the bile and rolls onto her back and takes a long, deep breath.

The sounds of explosions drift away, and a slow falling sensation overtakes her. Now, it is quiet, except for the sound of her own heavy breathing.

Get up, damn it!

My body...

Forget your pain. Logan needs you.

I can't.

Yes, you can! Get up! Now!

A tremor passes through her body and Jasmyn opens her eyes. She rolls onto one side and manages to push herself up to her knees. Once her eyes come into focus, she searches through the smoke and spots Caderyn a couple of feet away.

Staying low to the ground, she crawls through a pool of blood and kneels at Caderyn's side. A look of total horror crosses Jasmyn's face when she sees the thick pipe piercing his torso and pinning him to the ground.

"Forgive me, Agatha." Caderyn lifts his left hand and reaches for Jasmyn's face. He caress her cheek. "Please, forgive me."

Jasmyn shakes her head. "I… I'm not—"

"My daughter—" He groans. "My sweet child. Forgive me for all that I have done."

"I'm not Agatha."

He coughs, blood spilling over at the side of his mouth. "You're Agatha's granddaughter. You're my kin, my blood. You… are… Agatha."

As the intense vibrations coming from Caderyn weaken, his aura fading with each short breath, Jasmyn pulls her stare away from Caderyn's eyes and gazes down at the frightful gash. She closes her eyes tight and concentrates on all the spells she's learned from Patricia in search of a healing spell, but she can't find one. She lifts her gaze and sees Logan several feet away, dragging himself forward.

When she looks back at Caderyn's face, she finds the same serene look that her grandmother wore the night she passed away. His left hand, which caressed her cheek seconds ago, splatters into the pool of blood as it falls limply to the ground. The vibrations cease. His aura vanishes.

"No!" Logan shouts as he reaches his arm out in vain for Caderyn. He rolls onto his back and screams as his body judders, slapping up and down on the concrete, his head and torso bouncing repeatedly against the floor. He screams once more before the last violent seizure breaks, leaving him weak and unconscious, his arms and legs sprawled out in surrender.

In the time it takes Jasmyn to stand, Kean appears at Logan's side, lifts him up into the air, and stabs him in the heart.

24

RETRIBUTION

The wail Jasmyn releases from deep within her lungs roars across the airport, over the sounds of burning wreckage, and into the hearts of the crowd of travelers and soldiers gathered at the outskirts of the airport. Her brother's perfect blue aura transforms into a dark gray, then misty white, and then nothing at all. Jasmyn drops to her hands and knees and sobs.

After seeing Kean stab Logan in the heart, Patricia picks up two thick metal beams from a pile of rubble and pierces them straight through Breccan's back. She lifts him in the air with the two beams and screams as she splits his torso in two. Dropping the beams, she looks back at Kean holding Logan's dead body and drops to her knees. She sinks lower, onto her hands, her body barely able to stay upright, her chest heaving with sorrow.

Arsen appears at her side. "You have very little time. You have to take Jasmyn and go." When she doesn't respond, he shakes her vigorously until he draws her out of her daze. He stares deep into her eyes. "Please. You have to go now! You still have Jasmyn. She still needs you."

Kean tosses Logan's dead body to the side and raises his arms as the clan's magic engulfs him. A ring made of solid black onyx materializes on the fourth finger of his right hand. His wounds instantly heal, and his muscles rejuvenate to their most powerful and youthful state. He is the new Foreman Clan leader, and with this comes a new set of rules—and new magic.

Once the magic has settled on Kean's form, he turns to

Patricia and Arsen huddled together. He smirks viciously and shouts from across the field, "Kill her!"

"Go," Arsen whispers to Patricia before rising to his feet. He frowns fiercely and shouts at Patricia once more. "Go! Now!" He steps back and away from Patricia, with his hands in tight fists, fighting his clan's magic. But the magic is immutable, and it supersedes Arsen's control. His green irises turn black, followed by the whites of his eyes; his tight fists fall open.

Patricia slowly rises to her feet. "Arsen?"

When Patricia sees Arsen's sea green eyes—the same green eyes that have been eager to assist her these past few days, that loved her centuries ago, and never stopped loving her—turn as black as an ominous raven, she knows she's lost him.

He raises his arms to strike her, to kill her.

She fights back with tears in her eyes and a heavy heart.

~ ~ ~

A gust of wind passes over Jasmyn as she moves to Logan's body. With tears streaming down her cheeks, she rolls Logan onto his back and places his hands across his torso, folded on his stomach, like her grandmother's were that night she found her in her bed. His hands are still warm, and she squeezes them one last time.

I should be where you are now, Logan. I should be dead, not you. Not Kat.

Jasmyn feels Kean glaring down at her with contempt from just a few feet behind. His hate claws at her, like jagged knives piercing at her skin and tearing at her muscles. His aura crushes her chest and tugs at her spine. He wants her dead, and she can feel it.

She uses all the energy she has left to ward off his

assault, fighting desperately to draw strength from happy memories of Logan and Kat.

"Your brother was weak, like Caderyn. A bright blue aura never ruled over this clan."

Jasmyn opens her eyes and glares at Kean as he walks over to Caderyn. He tucks his button-down shirt neatly into his pants and pulls at the ends of a sleeve to straighten the fabric. He combs his fingers through his hair and scowls down upon Caderyn's body.

"For centuries, our clan lived by our magic, by our strength, our power. We took what we wanted. We never negotiated. Until Caderyn became our leader."

He spits in Caderyn's face, and then turns to face Jasmyn. He pulls out a dagger and unbuttons one of his shirt sleeves to roll it up.

"Peace, unity with your coven—Logan would have wanted the same," Kean snarls. "Or some other form of degradation that would have further decimated our clan. These desires are the weaknesses of mortals."

Jasmyn looks down upon her dead brother and closes her eyes once more.

Just do it. End it. Please.

"And what has striving for peace brought us? We were once great, and we've been reduced to nothing. Caderyn's desire for peace almost annihilated our clan."

Jasmyn opens her eyes and lifts her head sharply as the perfect string of thoughts unravels in her mind. She knows that in her weakened and inexperienced state she's no match against Kean's magic. He's a centuries-old sorcerer, wise in magic, and now the strongest member of the Foreman Clan. She also knows Finna's coven was never a match against the Foreman Clan's magic and their aggression. The only reason the Foreman Clan

183

was defeated, practically annihilated, was because of the Gregorn Dragons.

With subtle motions, she raises her left arm and whispers a spell.

"You're wrong." Jasmyn stands up and faces Kean.

"Am I?" Kean smiles and rolls up the other sleeve.

Repetitive crashing sounds to the side catches his attention. He finds two backpacks ripped open, their contents spread on the ground. A wooden box tumbles toward him and ceases rolling at his feet. It lands with its lid wide open, displaying its emptiness.

"It wasn't Caderyn's actions that annihilated your clan."

A monstrous, piercing roar in the sky pulls Kean's attention upward. His eyes widen as he gasps, "No!"

"It was the Gregorn Dragons."

As the enormous red dragon dives down toward him, Kean drops his blade and raises his hands to execute a shield spell. Baronyx's spray of fire bounces off Kean's shield, shoving Kean into the ground, his heels digging a deep groove in the concrete. Baronyx spreads his wings to decelerate, and Kean tumbles backward off his feet. The airport trembles when Baronyx lands; his roar pushes Kean back even further.

Kean grits his teeth and lifts his arms toward the dragon. Fire, wind, earth—Kean shoots the totality of his supernatural force toward Baronyx, as he did when he last faced the dragons long ago. He lifts concrete and slams it against Baronyx's body, torching his skin with bursts of fire, and blowing tornado-like winds down and around his frame. Baronyx flaps lazily up when Kean creates fissures in the ground, and lands easily next to them, watching Kean squirm with fear.

After several minutes of executing magic at his fullest strength, Kean collapses to the ground, debilitated. Blood drips from his nose and a rusty taste forms in his mouth. His muscles tremble with pain, and he is unable to rise to his feet. Once the smoke and dusts settle, Kean's lift his head to find the red dragon glaring down upon him.

Baronyx is unharmed.

Jasmyn stands with her hands in fists, ready to command Baronyx.

Without a moment to waste, Kean yanks Arsen from his fight with Patricia to stand between him and the red beast. Cowering behind the shield of Arsen's body, Kean breaks Arsen's trance and commands him, "Talk to them! Tell them to let us go."

It takes Arsen a few seconds to catch up to the current situation. He glances at Patricia to his right, then at the dragon towering over them, then over to Jasmyn at his left, standing guard over Logan's body. He smirks toward the ground before turning around to face Kean.

"I believe we are at their mercy, Kean. What would you have me do?"

Kean snatches his blade off the ground, slices Arsen's hand and his own, and then pulls Arsen in for a handshake. "Our blood is bound to be as one. Your life is given, my death undone. We are alive and dead as one."

Arsen curses at Kean, and then whips his hand out of Kean's grasp.

Kean grabs the front of Arsen's shirt. "If you don't convince them to let us go, this dragon will end the both of us. You have a connection with them. Convince them!"

Arsen snarls, sighs, and then nods before glancing over to Jasmyn.

Step away, Arsen. Baronyx will spare you.

Arsen sighs. *It won't matter. Kean has bound our lives*

185

with a life-blood spell. If you kill him, I die as well.

Jasmyn gasps.

You must tell Baronyx to kill him. He will continue to use me as a shield, a bargaining chip. It's his only power against you now. He has nothing else.

I... I can't.

You must.

"What is she saying?" Kean pulls Arsen close. "Tell me what she said!"

Arsen sighs. "Jasmyn wants me to get out of the way so Baronyx can kill you."

"Insolent child." A triumphant smirk appears on Kean's face. "I have bound our life forces. If I die, so will Arsen. The only way for Arsen to live is if we are both set free. Either we both live, or we both die. You decide."

"Damn it, Arsen!" Patricia yells.

With a heartwarming sting, he shrugs and gives her a hint of a smile.

How do we fight this? She presses her lips tight.

Oh, now you let me into your head? You have utterly poor timing.

Arsen!

You can't. Baronyx must kill him.

No. You'll die.

It's a valid sacrifice, even under your terms.

We'll think of something else. We'll entrap him!

Have you forgotten? Finna already tried that with Caderyn. Kean is too powerful now. He shakes his head. *He will always be after Jasmyn. He will never let it go. Without me, he has no power over you or Jasmyn. It's the only way out. It has to end.*

Patricia glances to the ground and then back at Arsen,

186

allowing sweeter moments from their youth, moments of their innocence and hopeful love affair, moments she had forgotten existed, to replay in her mind for Arsen to see. Holding hands for hours, long walks along the hillside, day-long embraces, passionate kisses, simpler times. Bittersweet tears fill her eyes; she knows Arsen is right.

Arsen inhales deeply as he reads her thoughts. He closes his eyes for a moment as his own memories generate warmth across his body. He's happy at the thought that Patricia still has so many good memories to recall.

Thank you, my love. Those were our best times.

Damn it, Arsen, I'm going to hate you forever for this.

Hopefully not.

"What are you doing?" Kean shouts to Arsen.

"I'm convincing them to fulfill my request."

"What did she say?"

"She's angry at me. She says she hates me, but she'll do what I ask. Now I just have to speak with Jasmyn."

Jasmyn shakes her head as soon as their eyes meet.

Please, don't ask me to do this.

You must. I'm already dead.

Please.

He'll never stop hunting you. You must continue on your mission. Besides, this isn't the end for me. My soul is safe with what I've done for you, with my last intentions. At least, I hope it is. Only the universe can decide.

"Make your decision, witch!"

Regardless, when you succeed and go back in time to before all this happened, find Patricia and speak well of me. The right corner of Arsen's lips curves upward. *Maybe things will be better the next time around.*

Jasmyn nods, swallows hard, and gives Baronyx the

order. She closes her eyes as Baronyx burns Arsen and Kean to ashes in one single blaze of dragon fire.

25

LEGACY

A violent burst of spring air blows from the east and scatters the two mounds of ashes into the cold night air, along with the acrid smell of incinerated flesh. When the wind ceases, as if announcing that it has completed its sorrowful task, Patricia lifts her head and opens her eyes to find only a black stain in the concrete where Arsen and Kean stood just moments earlier. The ashes are gone.

She kept her eyes closed during the execution, wanting to preserve her last image of Arsen, the hint of a smile hiding under those apologetic green eyes. She lowers her head to recite a death prayer, tears flowing down her cheek. After mourning the love that once was, Patricia stands up, wipes her face, and walks past Baronyx and over to Jasmyn.

Sitting obediently on his hind legs, Baronyx studies the scene carefully. He monitors Patricia as she walks over to Jasmyn who is sobbing over the dead body of a young man with a dagger sticking out of his chest. When his eyes reach Jasmyn, he concentrates and invades her thoughts.

He is your brother, Baronyx states in a baritone inner voice followed by a chuff.

Jasmyn nods with her head hanging low. *He was.*

You've lost both of your siblings now. Katarina and Logan.

Jasmyn nods again.

You could not save them.

189

No, I couldn't.

Baronyx exhales through his nostrils as he watches Patricia place her arm around Jasmyn. Both cry silently.

They were Foreman sorcerers, were they not?

Yes.

Baronyx growls. *Then you have summoned me to protect your coven once more. Now that I have fulfilled my task, please send me back to my prison.*

Jasmyn tilts her head to look up at Baronyx. *You want to go back?*

It is where I can dream and be with my brothers again.

In your dreams?

Better in my dreams than never at all.

A dream world where dead siblings continue to live is a world Jasmyn knows well. And the pain of waking up and acknowledging her sister no longer lives in the real world is something she can never get used to. And now, her brother is gone.

Jasmyn is alone, like Baronyx. But, unlike Baronyx who can never die and join his siblings, Jasmyn can.

I can't let you go back just yet. There's one more thing I need you to do.

Baronyx listens to Jasmyn's thoughts wander into the idea of commanding Baronyx to end her life. He stomps his feet and releases a low grumble. *You cannot command such a thing from me!*

Patricia stands to face Baronyx. "What's happening?"

"Nothing." Jasmyn lowers her gaze away from Baronyx. *I haven't decided on anything yet.*

He stomps his foot once more, harder, and growls. *There is no decision to make!*

With her hands straight up, Patricia puts up a shield and

prepares for a strike. "Jasmyn?" She breathes heavily as the brute creature glares down at her.

"He won't harm us. I have him under my control."

Jasmyn takes a moment to stare at her brother's dead body, at his peaceful face, and squeezes his hands one last time before standing up. *I'll see you and Kat soon.*

Baronyx huffs once more. *Agatha would never have asked me to do this.*

I'm not Agatha.

Yes, you are. You are her kin.

She steps over to Caderyn's body and stares down at his face. With his eyes closed and his face at peace, she realizes how similar he looks to Logan. His body lays twisted before her, and Jasmyn feels the urge to align it as she did with Logan's body. She kneels down and straightens Caderyn's torso.

I was never worthy of being her kin. I'm not worthy of being anyone's kin. I should have died. Not Kat. Not Logan. Me.

She unbends Caderyn's legs and places them flat on the ground. When she releases his pant leg, she stands and examines Caderyn's body, finding his arms splayed to the sides. Tears well up in her eyes as the atonement she's hoping for continues to elude her. She must continue, she must set his body at peace—a feeble attempt at gratitude for his efforts to save Logan.

Baronyx puffs smoke through his large nostrils. *What would Katarina think of your decision?*

After pausing for a moment at Baronyx's words, Jasmyn kneels once more and lifts Caderyn's left arm to place it on his torso.

Katarina would never have wanted you to do this. She would've wanted you to continue living.

Jasmyn stands up and shouts at Baronyx. "To do what, exactly?" She turns to Patricia who stares at her dumbfounded.

"To execute a spell I know nothing about? That no one knows how to execute? On an island that is nowhere to be found?"

She looks down at Logan, gasping to fight back sobs and then back up at Patricia.

"Why choose Logan to inherit Caderyn's magic, and then have him murdered? Why have Arsen help us get this far, only to have him die? It doesn't make sense! None of it makes sense! Why choose us only to have us fail? Our magic, the Foreman Clan's magic... it's all for nothing. Logan is dead! Kat is still dead! And I'm..."

She glances up at Baronyx with pleading eyes, and then back at Patricia. After a long, deep breath, she resumes control of herself and glances down at Logan and then Caderyn. "Please, just leave me alone while I set Caderyn right, and when I'm done," she looks up at Baronyx, "I'm going to end it all."

"End what?" Patricia demands. "Jasmyn?"

Shaking her head, wiping her face, Jasmyn kneels down on Caderyn's side and reaches for his right arm. She doesn't look at Patricia.

"What are you going to end?"

With a tug at the sleeve of his jacket, Jasmyn lifts his right arm and places it across his chest. She grabs both his hands in a fold and squeezes them gently as she squeezed Logan's hands just moments earlier, her tears spilling onto his hands as they did onto Logan's.

And before she gives Baronyx her final command, Jasmyn's knees give out, and she falls to the side unconscious.

~ ~ ~

Moments later, or so it seems, Jasmyn opens her eyes and finds herself lying in a bed in a hospital room. She turns to the side and sees Patricia sleeping on a chair. "Patricia?"

Patricia wakes up and stands. "Hey there."

"Where am I?"

"You're in St. John's Hospital, under observation. But, you're fine, physically at least."

Looking about the hospital room, Jasmyn tries to figure out her current situation. She notices tubes jutting out of her arm and follows them back to their connected machines.

"What's the last thing you remember?"

"Baronyx... Caderyn... Logan," her eyes shoot up at Patricia. "Is Logan..." Her throat swells up, preventing her from saying the words.

Patricia nods and swallows hard. "Yes. Logan's gone."

Her eyes well up, but something tells Jasmyn that now is not the time to cry. She blinks back the tears as images of lifeless bodies appear in her mind. "Caderyn is dead. Kean and," she glances up at Patricia, "Arsen too."

Patricia nods again, lowering her gaze.

"I'm so sorry."

A silent moment passes. "What else do you remember?"

She recalls the softness of Logan's dead hands as she held them tightly in her grip, crying into them and wishing to exchange places with him. She wanted to pull the dagger out of his heart and stab it into her own, but her coven's magic stopped her. And, after she had remembered that fact, she recalls how she was ready to command Baronyx to kill her.

Jasmyn gasps. "Where's Baronyx?"

"He's waiting for you at the airport."

"Waiting for me?" Jasmyn blinks wildly.

"He's been there for two days."

"Two days?" Jasmyn's eyebrows shoot upwards. "I've been in this hospital for two days?"

"Yes. He's waiting for you to return. It's quite chaotic over there. We had a hard time reassuring the authorities that as long as you're alive the dragon poses no harm, even after the military tried to make him move. They're no match for him."

"So, he's just sitting there, waiting, for me?"

"We're all waiting for you—Baronyx, Regina, me, and Gustavo."

At that very moment, Jasmyn realizes her uncle had to send Logan home in a coffin. She becomes numb as Logan's bruised face flashes in her mind, alongside Kat's battered cheeks the last time she saw her alive, Kat begging for her mother just before she passed, and Logan screaming in pain before Kean killed him. She lived through it all. She was there, and she couldn't save them.

She presses her eyes shut. *It's not my fault. None of it is my fault!*

Although she repeats the words in her head several times, a spiral of guilt pulls her inward. She descends further into self-pity, building a surge of self-hatred ready and willing to burn her alive. She presses her eyelids tight with her hands, fighting against the need to punish herself for her ineptitude and for surviving when she should have died.

I'm supposed to be dead. It should have been me.

"Jasmyn!" Patricia yells as she shakes Jasmyn's shoulders. "You have to stop that!"

Jasmyn's eyes open wide and meet Patricia's.

"Stop sinking!"

Jasmyn slaps Patricia's hands away and crosses her arms. She turns her head to the side, avoiding Patricia's stare, and blinks back tears.

"I know you're suffering—your aura is crystal clear. I, of all people, know what you're going through. Trust me." She sighs. "At the airport, before you passed out, you were ready to make an enormous mistake. It saddens me that you reached that point. It truly breaks my heart."

Patricia fights a grimace and then calms the worried lines on her face. "We were both there, Jasmyn. We both failed to save them. And we both survived."

They stare at one another for a quiet moment. Jasmyn opens her mouth to apologize, but Patricia lifts her hand to stop her from speaking.

"After giving it some thought these past few days, I realized that you hit rock bottom. That was the lowest point you'll ever reach, and you survived. And that's a good thing."

"It is?"

Patricia nods. "Because, once you reach rock bottom, the only way you can go from there is up."

"It doesn't feel like I'm going up. More like sideways."

A know-it-all smirk appears on Patricia's face. "Trust me. The fact that we're talking about it is evidence that we're already on our way up. The fact that I talked you out of your self-pity dive in two seconds is proof that you're getting stronger against its pull." She nods and releases a profound sigh of relief. "Now you have to learn how to use that pain and anger to propel yourself forward."

"How?"

"By having a goal in mind. Like…"

Patricia lifts her eyebrows for a few seconds before Jasmyn catches on.

"The time-reversal spell."

"Right."

"I can execute it. I can undo everything." Jasmyn eyes widen with hope, but then her shoulders slump as soon as she recalls one important detail. "None of us knows how to execute it."

After straightening the blanket on Jasmyn's bed, Patricia sits by Jasmyn's feet. "Arsen mentioned that Ryland was researching how to execute the time-reversal spell. Maybe we'll pay him a visit in Manchester."

"What about finding the Isle of Enid? We have to execute the spell on the island."

"Maybe Ryland has the answer to that as well. And, maybe he can answer a few more questions for us, like what happened to you the past few days. Or... maybe you can tell me."

Jasmyn furrows her eyebrows. "Tell you what?"

"You've been asleep for two whole days. We couldn't wake you. Medically, there was nothing wrong with you. You were just, sleeping. Even my magic wasn't penetrating your shield."

As her eyes search around the room, Jasmyn tries to recall the very last thing she remembers. "I was next to Caderyn's body, and then... I'm here in this bed."

"Something definitely happened to you. Do you feel different?"

Jasmyn shakes her head.

"Did you dream while you were asleep?"

She blinks a dozen times. "I was falling off a cliff. I was about to hit the ground, and then... I don't know... I just woke up."

"I thought you had vivid dreams?"

"I do, but this time..." She shrugs her shoulders.

Unsatisfied with Jasmyn's answer, Patricia shakes her head and stands. "Look at your right hand."

When Jasmyn raises her arm and splays out her fingers, she sees a skinny, solid black ring around her fourth finger. "It's a ring."

Patricia rolls her eyes. "Yes, I know. Try to take it off."

Upon sliding it up past her fingernail, the ring disintegrates into black dust and disappears. A new solid black ring materializes at the base of her fourth finger.

Jasmyn gasps softly. "What does that mean?"

"That looks exactly like the onyx ring Caderyn wore. If I had to guess, I'd say it means you, somehow, inherited Caderyn's magic. You are his kin after all, and you did kill Kean."

"Baronyx killed Kean."

"And Baronyx is under your control." Patricia shrugs her shoulders. "But that's just my guess. What would you make of it?"

As Jasmyn stares down at the solid black ring, twirling it around her finger, she concentrates on her dream. She leans back in her bed and closes her eyes, trying hard to remember if anyone was on the cliff. Was she pushed? Did she jump off willingly? She recalls the exact blue hue of the morning sky and the wind grazing her cheeks as she plummeted to her death. She tries to play it backwards—falling *up* the cliff, walking through a garden pathway, stepping out of a large house, and seeing sadness in Caderyn's eyes.

She gasps as the details of her dream clarify.

~ ~ ~

In the middle of a rectangular wooden dining table stands a metal candelabra with five lit candles. The room is pitch-dark, except for the dancing flames and a hint of a face illuminated at one end of the table. Jasmyn sits at the other end of the table and meets Caderyn's pensive gaze.

197

The whip of the candle's fire is threatened by a cool, gentle breeze. Jasmyn turns her head side to side in search of a window, but she can't see anything in the darkness.

She turns back to Caderyn. "Where are we?"

Caderyn lifts his gaze up toward the ceiling. Within a second, a large wooden chandelier with dozens of candles lights up the room. "This is where we lived."

"You and Finna?"

He nods and lowers his eyes to the base of the candelabra. "And Agatha."

After a pause, Jasmyn pushes her chair back and stands from her seat. As she walks around the room, her eyes gaze up at the thick wooden beams set across the ceiling and over to the woodwork along the wall panels. With her fingertips, she traces the detailed carvings on the beam in the center of the open space. When she looks back at the dining table, she sees the candles have all burned out, and lines of smoke swirl upwards from the wicks.

The smell of wood and ashes fills the air, along with the scent of fresh-cut flowers. She looks around and finds several wooden and metal urns with red roses and bright yellow daffodils. A white orchid with pink spots stands in its own tall metal vase at the center of a corner table. Jasmyn leans in to inhale the aroma.

"She loved flowers," Caderyn says.

Jasmyn notices the door to a room left wide open, as if inviting her in. She looks back at Caderyn, wondering if he intended for her to go inside.

He nods, and Jasmyn proceeds.

White blankets spill off a large bed. Empty drawers from a wooden cabinet sit on the ground, some upside down, some broken. A three-tiered jewelry box on top of a dresser has its three drawers pulled out halfway with some of its contents spilled out in front of a mirror.

A sting hits her stomach, and Jasmyn frowns as she realizes this is how Finna left their bedroom before running away with Agatha. The memory is so clear that she can smell the yellow tulips sitting in a vase on top of the dresser.

Jasmyn walks out of the room and finds Caderyn still seated at the dining table. She shakes her head as she realizes what Caderyn must have suffered. *What would Dad have done if one day Mom left him, took us with her, and never returned? Dad would have been devastated.*

Another soft breeze flows in and pushes the door of another room open. Just past the doorway, Jasmyn bends down to pick up a pink rag doll dressed in a white frock, with two brown, thick-threaded pony tails jutting from the top of its head. She passes her thumb over the two button eyes and along the stitching of the doll's lips. It's not smiling but not frowning either.

"That was Agatha's favorite." Caderyn clears his throat.

Jasmyn inspects the rag doll, pushing back its ponytails with long thumb strokes. After a moment, she steps into the room and finds pink and white blankets tossed off the bed and cabinet drawers emptied out onto the floor. A box of wooden toys lies on its side with its colorful blocks tumbled about. Above the bed, she sees a shelf with six colorful rag dolls sitting side by side, leaning against each other, their faces staring downward as if mourning the loss of their playmate.

"There's one more room."

She walks out of Agatha's bedroom.

Caderyn points to a closed door. "Over there."

With the rag doll in hand, Jasmyn heads over and turns the knob on the door. It creaks when she opens it, as if warning her of what she'll find. Inside the room she sees paintings, human-size sculptures, large gold medallions, and other artifacts hanging on hooks along the right wall. Thick drapes of complex weaving, heavy bear pelts, and white lion skins hang over large wooden bars on the left side. A large coat with wolf fur covering the back sits on a tall, broad-shouldered mannequin.

As Jasmyn steps through the middle path, a large wooden chest with its lid flipped wide open catches her eye. When she arrives at the chest, she looks inside and sees a black satin cushion at the bottom.

"What was in the box?" Jasmyn calls toward the door of the room.

"Dragon eggs."

Jasmyn inhales deeply.

"The ones Finna stole."

At that moment, as she gazes down at the empty chest, Jasmyn knows the betrayal Caderyn felt. The anger and sorrow that consumed him back then now burrows through her heart, and she grabs her shirt and closes her eyes. Finna proved to be a liar and a thief. She betrayed him. She drugged him, kept him asleep while she stole his most valuable treasures—his daughter, his dragons, and his sanity.

She tugs her shirt more tightly as each breath fills her lungs to their fullest capacity. Tears drip down to the ground, and she finds it hard to swallow. Caderyn's intense rage traverses her body as she recalls the fire he created that destroyed their home. Every evidence of their happiness was gone. He was no longer the Caderyn that lived there. That Caderyn died in the flames.

"No!" Jasmyn shouts, shaking her head. She slams the lid of the chest shut and storms out of the treasure room. "It won't work!"

"What won't work?"

"You're trying to change my mind about you." She walks to the table and points toward the floor. "You want me to feel what you felt. You want me to sympathize with you. It won't work."

Caderyn wrinkles his forehead as he rises from his seat. "I want you to understand why I did what I did. It wasn't just an act of power, or a trivial decision made from lust for revenge." He rises from his seat. "Pure agony, infidelity, complete loss... will drive any person to do the most unthinkable."

Jasmyn glares at Caderyn for a moment before he continues.

"You were about to take your life just now, weren't you?"

Her lips part, and she gasps quietly. She lowers her gaze. Feeling utterly exposed, she stands silently and stares at the ground.

"So, you know what I speak of." He takes a step to the side. "The day Finna took Agatha from me, the day she stole my dragon eggs, the day she proved all those claims to be true, was the last day I was alive. My true self, the Caderyn that Finna knew, that loved her and Agatha to the ends of the universe, died that day."

Caderyn walks to a console that holds a small statue of a couple holding hands with a little girl in pigtails. "See this?" He raises the sculpture for Jasmyn to see. "The little girl is gazing up at her mother, and the mother down upon the child. Both smiling. And what is the father doing? He, too, gazes upon the child."

He places the sculpture back down on the console. "I wanted a son." He looks up at Jasmyn. "I loved Agatha with all my heart, she was the world to me, but... she was never truly mine. She was Finna's child."

"She was your child too."

He shakes his head and glances at the floor. "She belonged to Finna. She belonged to the coven." He looks back up at Jasmyn. "Did you know we tried to have more children?"

"I didn't know."

"We tried for a long time. That was one of the reasons the council was in such an uproar. I had no heir. They wanted a guarantee that Agatha would not take over the clan." He shakes his head and huffs. "Such were the times…"

He heads to an open door that leads to the rear of the house. "Shall we take a stroll?"

After a moment of hesitation, Jasmyn follows Caderyn out to a garden filled with overhanging trees and pathways lined with flowerbeds of various colors. Rosebushes stand tall to the right of the pathway and fills the air with a sweet aroma.

Caderyn pulls a pink stem up to his nose. "I've missed that smell."

Jasmyn breathes in the flowery scent as she sees faint images of baby Agatha hobbling along the very path they walk, giggling as her mother chases her. She stops for a moment and is mesmerized by the delightful scene, by the happy sounds of laughter. When the imagery vanishes, Jasmyn continues behind Caderyn.

They arrive at a tall hedge with an iron gate that leads them to a cliff overlooking a valley of rolling green hills. Caderyn steps through the gate first and then gestures for Jasmyn to follow. When Jasmyn steps onto the cliff, she stands alongside of Caderyn and peeks over the edge.

"When Finna left me, Agatha was very small—too small to remember me. Twenty years passed before I saw my daughter again. By then, Agatha was an adult, a trained sorceress, a skilled warrior. I sent a clansman wearing my face as a disguise to meet her, and she killed him believing it was me. She killed her own father."

"Why would you do that?"

He chuckles. "It's true what they say—hope is both man's greatest strength... and his greatest weakness."

"I don't understand."

"I needed to know for sure if I had completely lost my daughter. I needed to know if Finna had brought Agatha up to hate me, or if Agatha had enough compassion to consider my side of the story. To my dismay, Agatha was no longer my daughter. She killed me without hesitation."

Jasmyn sucks in a breath as a tight pressure forms in her lungs. She places her hand flat against her chest as bile rises in her throat. She grits her teeth as she feels what Caderyn felt upon learning that Agatha killed Doran, believing it was him. Her heart burns with grief.

"Stop that. Stop making me feel what you felt."

Caderyn faces Jasmyn. "I can't stop it."

She drops to one knee, pressing her hand harder against her ribs. As tears stream down her cheeks, she fights the overwhelming pain passing through her body. It dissipates into a weak numbness, and Jasmyn glares up at Caderyn once more.

"I'm not doing this to you."

"Then who is?"

Caderyn huffs and turns to face the cliff edge, leaning over to look down below.

"I've had many children in my lifetime, but I never recognized any one of them as my kin. It's not something you control, you know. In our clan, it just happens. Call it irrational, like love. No one knows how or why a certain person falls in love with another; there is no formula—they just do. Similarly,

203

no one knows how a sorcerer selects a kin, an heir, they just do."

Still glaring at Caderyn, Jasmyn rises to her feet.

"I often wondered why it was that Finna and I couldn't have any more children after Agatha. We were both healthy. Nothing natural was in the way. But, after all that's occurred, I believe I know why."

She narrows her eyes. "Why?"

"When Finna and I married, I believe our powers joined together into one new entity. And, as it is with our kind, there can only be one heir to inherit this new magic. There was no need for more children; Agatha was meant to inherit both Finna's power and my own."

Jasmyn shakes her head.

"And now, you will inherit my magic."

Remembering the last time she and Logan spoke to each other, defying the existence of magic, practically cursing at it, Jasmyn shakes her head. "I don't want your magic. I didn't want Nana's magic, or Finna's. I don't want any of it!"

A hefty gust of wind blows up the mountainside and slams against Jasmyn's body, picking her up and sending her over the cliff's edge. Caderyn grabs her by the wrist and squeezes as her body is whipped upwards and out, as if it's being sucked into the sky. She feels the wind scraping against her face, tugging at her dress and pulling on her legs. She screams as Caderyn's grip weakens, his nails digging into her arm so sharply that it tears the skin.

This isn't real. Jasmyn forces her eyes open and screams at the horrific drop below her. *It's a dream. It's just a dream. It's just a goddamned dream. I'll wake up soon. No. I want to wake up now. Wake up now, damn it! Wake! Up!*

"It's not up to you," Caderyn shouts as her hand slips through his hold.

It's a dream. None of it is real. I control my dreams. Stop it. Stop blowing!

Jasmyn inhales and holds her breath. When she exhales, she shouts, "Enough!"

The wind suddenly stops, and Jasmyn's body drops over the cliff's edge with Caderyn still maintaining his grip. Her body slaps the jagged side of the cliff, the rock jabbing her ribs and shoulders. A hard knock on the back of her head shoots bolts of pain through her entire body. She yelps at the stabbing sensations, at the pounding in her head.

This isn't real. Please. This isn't real!

Caderyn lowers his body to the ground to strengthen his hold, spreading his legs wide behind him. He stares down at her, but he doesn't pull her up.

Jasmyn shakes her head wildly. "Don't let me go."

"It's not up to me," Caderyn whispers. "No one can control magic's will."

He releases his grip and Jasmyn falls to the valley below, screaming at the top of her lungs.

Stop falling! Stop! Now!

Katarina and Logan's faces flash before Jasmyn's eyes, followed by happy visions of Caderyn with Finna and a baby Agatha. She continues to fall, sobbing at the thought of her life ending, of never fixing what she broke, of never making it up to Katarina or Logan.

This can't be how it ends. It has to stop. Please! Stop!

As soon as her body hits the ground, her screaming ceases, and everything is quiet once more.

~ ~ ~

"Wow." Patricia takes a deep breath once Jasmyn

finishes telling her dream. She shrugs her shoulders. "I guess you're Caderyn's heir."

Jasmyn looks down at her onyx ring, spinning it in its place. "I guess so."

"Have you inherited his memories?"

She nods.

"Do you remember Finna and Agatha, when she was young."

"I do." Jasmyn smiles for a moment as images of a chubby baby Agatha appear in her mind. Then, she recalls her last dream and the smile disappears. "It's all so sad, the way things turned out. You can't blame Finna or Caderyn."

Patricia sits back in a chair and sighs.

The hospital room door opens and a nurse walks in pulling medical equipment. The wheels on the white device squeak as she moves to Jasmyn's side of the room. "I'm going to check your vitals."

As the nurse wraps the blood-pressure band around Jasmyn's arm, she hums a soothing melody. Jasmyn leans her head back, closes her eyes, and concentrates on the song. She wanders through all the fresh memories she's inherited from Caderyn. They appear one by one, in no particular order, like a photo collage of special moments from his life. The images traverse centuries, cultures, and countries.

Jasmyn opens her eyes at a particular memory as it gradually flows in. She lifts her head as she recalls Caderyn on a boat in the middle of the Northern Seas. Violent waves rock the boat, and crisp winds move thick gray clouds overhead, dropping pellets of water and ice upon them. Caderyn stares out at an island far away—the Isle of Enid. Jasmyn gasps as she watches Caderyn pass the dagger across his hand and cast a spell.

As the nurse rolls the machine out of the room, Patricia

stands. "What is it?"

It takes Jasmyn a few seconds to snap out of her daze. She looks down at her hands and then up at Patricia and speaks slowly. "Caderyn hid the Isle of Enid. He used a blood spell to cloak it."

Patricia's eyes open wide.

"I know exactly where it is."

26

DISHONORED

"I don't understand." Oregon struggles with the *Book of Sol* as he steps down to the street. The ancient book's enormous square shape feeling heavy in his old arms. "What do you mean you haven't seen anything?"

Ryland slams the door to his chambers for the last time and walks to the large truck where movers are organizing boxes full of his belongings. A man with a clipboard directs two other men who are picking up boxes full of books, scrolls, computers, relics, and other possessions.

"The visions have stopped. I would get at least ten visions a day, from various angles, from different people and occurrences around the world." He shoves the ring of keys into his side pocket. "Since the annihilation of the Foreman Clan two days ago, I've seen nothing."

"Maybe there's nothing to see."

"There is always something to see. There is always something happening in the world. I can't control how or when the visions come, but they always come. Some are more trivial than others, inconsequential to anything really, but they come to me, every day, multiple times a day. And now, nothing."

"What was your last vision?"

When one of the movers fumbles a long, rectangular wooden carton, Ryland shouts, "Be careful with that box!"

All the workers freeze and look up at Ryland.

Ryland inhales deeply to regain his composure.

"Please," he says in a calmer tone, "be careful with it. It's very valuable."

The man with the clipboard nods and directs the other two to wrap the wooden crate with extra padding and bubble wrapping. Ryland returns to Oregon's side and takes the *Book of Sol* from his hands, alleviating his old friend of the burden.

"As you saw on the news, the red dragon obliterated the Foreman Clan, reducing Kean and Arsen to ashes. They are done. As the news helicopters flew around to the other side of the airport, do you recall seeing Jasmyn on her knees next to Caderyn?"

Oregon nods. "She fainted."

"Right. Once Jasmyn fainted, lightning flashed before my eyes. Images from the battles between the Foreman Clan and Finna's coven replayed in my mind, shuffling about, like a dealer with a deck of cards mixing them all out of order. And Jasmyn was in there, in those memories, with Caderyn."

"How is that possible?"

"I don't know. There was one more lightning flash and then... nothing." He glances at Oregon. "I haven't received a single new vision since."

Ryland huffs when he notices the number of boxes still sitting on the sidewalk. He urges the movers to pick up the pace.

Oregon looks both ways down the street. He leans in close to Ryland. "Are you in some sort of danger? Is this why we're leaving in such a hurry?"

"We're leaving because the Foreman Clan no longer exists, and I have no protection."

"From what do you need protecting?"

"Jasmyn and Patricia."

Oregon tilts his head. "Why do you fear them?"

A wry smile appears on Ryland's face. "I was the one

who convinced Finna to leave Caderyn. I advised her to steal those dragon eggs from Caderyn's family. I helped her escape off the island with Agatha. And, I was the one who exposed Finna's treachery to the clan so that Caderyn would be forced to attack the coven."

Oregon widens his eyes. "You started the war with the coven."

"I did. I had to. The clan was on the brink of revolution. Kean and Granger had been riling up the clansmen against Caderyn for some time. That kind of instability in those times would have weakened us, made us vulnerable to other clans looking for an opportunity to conquer us. Creating a common enemy united the men and unified the clan."

As he scratches his white, wiry beard with his right hand, Oregon twirls these new facts around in his head. "So, you believe Jasmyn will kill you for starting the war? Do you think she's capable of such a thing?"

"I don't know what she knows or what she's capable of. I can't rely on the fickle nature of sorcerers. And since my visions have abandoned me, there is no way to find out their next step or their intentions. All I know is I'm without protection."

Oregon nods and swings his arms behind him, his right hand grabbing hold of his left wrist. "You have much to worry about."

The movers finish loading all of the boxes except for one, his most precious cargo. When all three movers lift the rectangular box covered in thick layers of bubble wrap, Ryland holds his breath until the box is safely loaded into the truck.

Oregon notices Ryland's concern. He leans in close. "What's in that container?"

Ryland walks to his car parked behind the truck. Oregon climbs into the passenger seat. "That, my old friend, is a gift for our new protector, Loritida."

Oregon narrows his eyes as he recalls the name. "Ah, yes. Loritida handed you the *Book of Sol*."

"That's right." Ryland starts the engine.

"But, why would she offer you protection? She was once part of Finna's coven, was she not?"

"Yes, until Finna exiled her. The coven was once under Loritida's control, but when she started dealing in dark magic, Finna gathered her sisters and revolted. It was a horrific battle. Loritida lost her mother, her five sisters and brothers, and her two daughters. Once it was over, Finna decided not to kill her. Instead, she cursed her to be barren and exiled her from the coven."

"Seems like a harsher punishment than death."

Ryland nods. "You see, old friend, even the most peaceful of people are capable of dark actions. Loritida wants revenge, and that I can work with. I don't know Jasmyn's intentions. You cannot trust a scorned sorceress."

The truck begins its journey, and Ryland drives out onto the road behind it. With his arms stretched in front of him, Oregon yawns as he prepares for his two-hour car ride.

"Before I attempt to go to sleep, would you be so kind as to set my mind at ease regarding the puzzle that's been rattling my brain for the past ten minutes. Please, tell me—what's in that last container?"

Ryland chuckles but doesn't answer.

"Please, you must tell me. I won't be able to sleep with my mind trying to solve this puzzle."

"Very well, Oregon. Five untouched Gregorn Dragon eggs."

Oregon stares at Ryland in awe, his mouth agape.

"Don't worry, my old friend. I'm giving Loritida only

one of those eggs. You never know what the future may hold."

~ End Of Book Two ~

ACKNOWLEDGMENTS

I'd like to thank my one and only brother for pushing me to finish The Onyx Ring. He was the first to read The Box Of Souls, in three sittings, and the first to read The Onyx Ring before releasing it out into the world. Bro, thank you for constantly nagging me and giving me the stink-eye whenever I gave you an excuse for the delay of this release. As the most avid science fiction and fantasy reader I know, your eagerness and support has meant the world to me.

I'd like to thank the incredible team at Quill Pen Editorial. Thanks to Catherine Jones Pane for slapping my manuscript straight across the face until I got it just right. Thanks to Stephanie and Benjamin for helping me clear out all the muck during line edits. And thanks to all three of you for all your critiques.

To Jenny Zemanek, the brilliant artist at Seedlings Design Studio, who worked through my uncouth, clumsy ideas and mock ups and made a gorgeous cover.

To my family who has patiently listened to my tireless rants on why it has taken so long to write the second book in the series, I thank you. To my cat who has been with us these past 3 years, thanks for making writing all that more difficult. If it wasn't for your incessant need to be petted each and every single time I sat at my laptop, this book would have been completed a lot sooner.

And finally, to everyone who chose to purchase my book, thank you a million times over. I hope you enjoyed reading it as much as I enjoyed writing it.

ABOUT THE AUTHOR

Tanya Miranda grew up daydreaming about everything. From human-looking aliens hiding in the government, to witches and dragons skulking in the shadowy corners of her basement, to finding the love of her life running through a hailstorm; her imagination never ceases to create kooky characters in the most bizarre circumstances. Her one true wish is to draw the images that materialize in her head. Until then, she'll continue to put her dreams into stories.

To find out more about the author's writing, visit her at
www.tanyamiranda.com